HER COWBOY'S WOUNDED HEART

COWBOY BROTHERS OF HART'S RIDGE RANCH SERIES

BOOK FIVE

FAITH LANDON

LET'S STAY IN TOUCH

Get the prequel to the **Cowboy Brothers of Hart's Ridge Ranch** series for FREE when you sign up for my reader email list! You'll also be the first to learn about my books, special content, promotions, and more.

FaithLandon.com

Are you on Facebook? Follow my author page to connect with me and other readers who love clean and wholesome cowboy romances.

facebook.com/FaithLandonAuthor

HER COWBOY'S WOUNDED HEART

Isaac Hart buried his dreams of love and family three years ago after the tragic loss of his wife and unborn child, finding solace only in the work that keeps his heart guarded and his mind focused. But when Tabitha Young—a gentle, resilient single mother—and her young son, Caden, arrive at Hart's Ridge Ranch for a special riding program, Isaac's world shifts in ways he never expected.

Drawn to Tabitha's kindness and the quiet strength she brings to every challenge, Isaac begins to feel a spark of hope he thought he'd lost forever. Tabitha is determined to build a safe, joyful life for her autistic son, and Isaac can't help but admire her courage in the face of her own struggles.

As Isaac and Tabitha's paths intertwine at Hart's Ridge Ranch, they must choose whether facing the past is worth the chance at a future that could heal both their wounded hearts—if they're brave enough to try.

The **Cowboy Brothers of Hart's Ridge Ranch** is a sweet contemporary western romance series with clean and wholesome stories about the blessings of family and the power of love.

Available in ebook and print.

Look for more novels in the series coming soon!

PROLOGUE

Three Years Ago

ISAAC HART LOVED the trip home. Whether he was driving back after running errands or other ranch business, or simply walking the short distance from his office in the stables to the small cabin he and his wife had to themselves at his family's sprawling property, Hart's Ridge Ranch, he was always happy as he headed home.

It was because of the feeling he got every time he put his hand on his front door. It was a feeling of peace. He was secure in the knowledge that Anna would be on the other side of the door, or that she soon would be after driving home herself from the school in Greenville where she taught seventh-grade English.

On that particular summer evening, Isaac walked home, his body coated with sweat after helping his older brother Jacob train a horse, and he imagined what waited for him.

Anna would smile in greeting, and they would chat about all of their hopes and dreams for their future while they cooked supper. Sometimes they ate up at the main house with the rest of Isaac's family, but most nights, especially recently, they savored their private meals alone in their cozy little home.

Isaac had met Anna five years ago at a local rodeo. She had been rifling through her purse to buy herself a cotton candy, her blonde hair flowing loose down her back in soft waves. Isaac had swooped in and paid before she even looked up. After talking to her for about two minutes, Isaac had fallen hard and fast for Anna. They had married the following year, neither of them wanting to waste any time before starting their life together.

And now they were expecting a child.

Isaac grinned, as he did every time he thought of it. Anna was having his baby. He was going to be a father.

With his heart swelling in his chest, Isaac opened the door and stepped inside the cabin.

Anna was lounging on the couch in the living room, one hand resting on her rounded stomach. She was almost eight months along and often said she felt like a beached whale. Isaac thought she had never been more beautiful.

She stirred and looked up drowsily as Isaac entered. His heart ached at the signs of exhaustion on her face. But then she smiled at him, and some of his worry eased. No matter what, his Anna always found a way to comfort him with her smile.

"Long day?" she asked.

"Probably not as long as yours," Isaac said.

Anna waved her hand. "I tried to do some laundry, then gave up and sat on the couch. I must've fallen asleep."

"I'll do the laundry later." Isaac bent down to kiss his wife.

He didn't mind picking up extra tasks around the house, whether or not Anna was pregnant.

It hadn't been an easy few months for her. Early on, she had suffered from horrible morning sickness, and now, in the third trimester, she had swollen feet and hands, and even the simplest tasks seemed to exhaust her.

But never once did she give in to being miserable. Anna, like Isaac, was just excited to welcome their child—girl or boy—into the world. They hadn't found out the gender from the doctor, although he had offered to tell them months ago. They both wanted to be surprised.

Anna's eyes were tender on him. "You are the best husband in the world, Isaac Hart."

He wanted nothing more than to sit down beside her and hold her in his arms for a while.

But his shirt was filthy from working with horses all day, and he was still coated in sweat and grime due to the oppressive heat.

"Don't get up," he told her. "I need a shower and fresh clothes, then I'll put together something for us to eat."

When he emerged, he found Anna had ignored his advice and was on her feet putting items for supper out on the counter. Isaac watched her pause as she set a tomato down on the cutting board.

His brow furrowed. She was moving slowly—even more so than usual—and there was obvious tension in her back.

"You okay?" He moved to her side, placing a gentle hand on her lower back.

Anna nodded her head up and down. "I'm fine. I just feel a bit odd."

"Odd, how?" Isaac surveyed her face closely. "Are you feeling pain?"

"No. Not now, anyway." Anna lifted one shoulder. "I felt a bit of pain earlier, but I think it was one of those mini contractions."

"Contractions?" Isaac's heart leapt with fear. The baby wasn't due for another month at least.

"I'm sure it's fine." Anna waved her hand and started to chop more vegetables for a salad. "The doctor says it's normal to experience a bit of cramping."

Isaac had read every book on pregnancy and parenting that Anna had brought home, so he knew it was normal. It didn't stop him from worrying as they shared a peaceful meal.

By bedtime, however, his worry had eased. Anna settled in beside him under the covers and smiled as her hand cradled her stomach.

Isaac read a book while he waited for Anna to drift off to sleep. He kept glancing down at her.

"I'm fine, I promise." She smiled, her eyes still closed. "I think she's just getting anxious to meet us."

"She?" Isaac set down his book.

Anna sighed dreamily. "I don't know for sure, but I just feel it's a girl. I can't explain why."

Stroking his wife's shoulder, Isaac grunted. He thought it might be easier to raise a son, but he would love a daughter too. He'd never had any sisters growing up. He knew his parents would be overjoyed to have a little girl to spoil rotten and dote on at the ranch. He smiled to himself as he imagined the joy a baby girl would bring to everyone in his family. Images of the future that might await him carried Isaac into a deep and pleasant sleep at Anna's side.

A few hours later, in the dark silence of the night, he jolted awake.

Anna was curled tight on her side next to him, moaning in agony.

Isaac moved to turn on the light, every inch of his body vibrating in a cold panic. Something was wrong. Something was very wrong.

"Anna." Isaac placed gentle hands on her shoulders. "Anna, what's happening?"

"It hurts," she whispered through gritted teeth. "I think I'm —" A violent moan rolled through her. "Isaac, we need to go to the hospital."

Isaac didn't pause to think, he just launched into movement. He pulled on his boots and a jacket, then carefully helped Anna to sit up in her nightgown and put on her own shoes.

Her face was pale and covered in a sheen of sweat. Isaac pushed his fear aside as he helped her out to his truck. He had never seen Anna's eyes so glazed and unfocused.

During the drive to the Greenville hospital, Anna tried to breathe in and out. Sometimes she would manage to relax slightly, but then after a few minutes, she would double over, clutching her abdomen.

"Is it contractions?" Isaac felt helpless. "Are you going into labor?"

"I don't know." Anna shook her head, her locks of hair sticking to her sweat-soaked neck. "I just know it hurts, and I feel—I feel something's going wrong."

"We'll be at the hospital soon." Isaac forced his voice to remain steady. "We're almost there. The doctors will know what to do."

At the hospital, Anna was whisked away in a wheelchair. Isaac followed, his heart pounding against his chest. Somehow, he managed to pull himself together enough to phone his mother and tell her where they were.

He held Anna's hand in the emergency center exam room as the nurses took her vitals and a physician came in to examine Anna. Isaac didn't like the grim look on the doctor's face.

His rising panic began to churn into an awful dread as the doctor said the baby was in distress and they had to act quickly. Anna needed to go to the operating room.

"It'll be okay," she whispered to him, strength in her eyes in spite of her own fears. Instead of him reassuring her, it was Anna who offered words of comfort to him while Isaac stood there, feeling as if his terrified heart were beating outside of his body.

Everything moved fast from there. Another round of pain racked Anna and she started to wail, the sounds unlike anything Isaac had ever heard. The only thing he could possibly compare it to was when he was ten, and he had seen a horse fall and break its front leg clean in two, the sharp white bone poking out. It had been in unimaginable pain. And now Anna was in such pain, and Isaac could do nothing to help. He clutched her hand and murmured over and over how much he loved her.

But then she was pulled away from him, wheeled off to an operating room.

Isaac was standing alone in the empty hallway outside when his mother showed up. She wasn't alone. His entire family had insisted on coming. Tom and Vera sat by Isaac's side, and Jacob, always ready to take charge of the situation, set off to find food. Liam and Mateo spoke quietly about how they were sure it would all be fine in the end. They even called

Beau and Sawyer, who were both traveling, to keep them in the loop.

At one point, a nurse with a haggard face came out, wisps of hair escaping her tight ponytail.

"Mr. Hart?" She placed a gentle hand on Isaac's shoulder. "She's still in surgery. We're doing our best."

Then she turned, quickly heading back to the operating room, while Isaac buried his face in his hands.

His family didn't leave him. No one faced anything alone in the Hart family. They comforted him, prayed with him, worried for both him and Anna.

And the baby they already loved so much.

The hours blurred together. It was one long nightmare, and Isaac kept hoping he would wake up from it and find himself lying back in bed beside his sleeping wife, but that wasn't to be.

The doctor emerged from the room and strode silently toward Isaac and his family. His grave face opened a pit of dread in Isaac's stomach.

Words seemed to reach Isaac's ears from far away, but he still understood them. The baby's heartbeat had been weak when they arrived. They tried to save it in surgery, but they were unsuccessful. As for Anna...

It was here that the doctor's words seemed to dry up before they reached Isaac's ears. They were too horrific to accept.

Anna was gone, too.

Isaac had lost both of them. His beloved wife. His cherished, unborn child.

Everything that mattered to him.

All gone now.

With a choked sob, his mother turned away.

Jagged grief ripped at Isaac, but he held it inside, trying to process the terrible news.

The doctor was still talking, but nothing made any sense as shock overwhelmed him. His mother was crying harder now. His brothers were staring at him with drawn faces. Even his father wore a look of indescribable anguish as Isaac met his sober gaze.

"I'm very sorry," the doctor said.

Woodenly, Isaac rose to his feet. His heart wanted to reject everything that was happening, but he couldn't. It was real. It was unimaginable, but it was real.

He wasn't going to get to hold Anna or their baby. They would never have the family they'd dreamed of and prayed for. Anna and the baby wouldn't be coming home with him. Not ever. They were both gone.

He watched in a state of numbness as the doctor retreated back down the hallway. Isaac's family gathered around him with words of comfort and sympathy, arms wrapping around him. He felt none of it. He heard nothing. Time itself seemed to slow to an agonizing halt as he struggled to absorb what was happening.

He didn't know how long it was before a nurse came out to gently ask if he wanted to spend a few moments with Anna and the baby in the operating room. He walked there alone, his cowboy boots thumping hollowly over the hospital floor tiles.

The room was quiet, sterile. The surgery team had cleaned it up, removed all evidence of the horror that had taken place there.

Anna lay on the table covered in a sheet up to her neck.

Their child appeared to be peacefully asleep in the nursery bed beside her, wrapped in a pale pink blanket.

It was a girl. Just like Anna had sensed it would be. A small, beautiful girl, perfect in every way except she wasn't breathing, and she never would.

Isaac stroked his daughter's delicate cheek, his gaze blurred by tears. He murmured soft words to her, then closed his eyes and prayed for God to watch over her now that she was in His hands.

He could only look at Anna's still body on the bed. He had so much he wanted to say to his wife—anything but goodbye.

Isaac could never forget the way she had looked up at him for the last time, dark bags beneath her exhausted eyes. He could never forget the pain she had endured in her final hours.

Right before she had been whisked away to the operating room, she had looked up at Isaac, and her colorless lips parted.

"I love you," Anna had whispered to him. "I always will."

It was as if she had known she wouldn't last the night. Isaac had hoped and prayed for everything to be all right, but Anna had already known it was over.

Isaac gently touched his fingers to her cold cheek. "I love you, too, my sweet Anna. I always will."

The doctors told him it was no one's fault. The labor had come early and with severe complications. In the end, Anna had lost too much blood, and her heart had failed.

But Isaac knew. If they had only gone to the hospital sooner. If they had lived just a little closer to town.

If he had been paying enough attention to his instincts to insist that something was wrong that evening, instead of waiting until Anna was in too much pain to ignore.

If there was any blame, it was his alone. He had failed her. He had failed their baby girl as well. Their pain was over now, but his was just beginning.

And he knew he was broken beyond repair.

CHAPTER 1

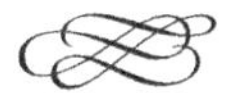

resent Day

Tabitha Young thought the Wyoming highway looked like it went on forever. She gripped the steering wheel with two hands as the car flew past miles and miles of green fields. In the distance, stunning mountains rose up against the wide blue sky.

She had never been to Wyoming, but the landscape took her back to her childhood in Utah and the long rides her father used to take her on when he was transporting horses to other ranches.

She had savored those trips. With four siblings, it was always a joy to have her father all to herself for just a few hours on the road.

Tabitha glanced in the rearview mirror to check on Caden, who was napping in his car seat in the back.

She smiled to herself. He was always so cute when he slept, his round cheeks smooth and his expression peaceful.

She had left San Francisco and embarked on the long drive to Hart's Ridge Ranch in Wyoming, all for him.

Tabitha just hoped the six-week program for autistic children at the ranch was as great as it had seemed on paper.

Caden was almost six, and Tabitha had gone to plenty of workshops, therapists, and special programs with him. Some were better than others, and Tabitha felt she had developed something of a stellar instinct.

Almost from the moment Caden was born, Tabitha had thrown herself into research. She'd consulted with countless doctors and therapists. She had combed through blogs and articles, and recently she had even started posting online herself about her and Caden's experiences, when she wasn't bogged down with her work as a website designer.

Most of the mothers of autistic children she knew didn't have jobs outside of caring for their kids, but Tabitha was a single mother. She needed to work, and she was lucky to have a job she could do from home.

Tabitha moved her eyes back to the road, and she felt a burst of nostalgia. How was Caden six already? It seemed like she had just been holding him as an infant in her arms.

It was her own childhood memories that brought on Tabitha's emotions; she was certain. She had loved her youth spent running wild at her family's ranch in Utah, and she had missed it. She wanted Caden to enjoy nature and animals as she had. That's why she'd started looking for a good outdoor program for her son. Caden's therapist agreed that he was getting to the age where working with animals and being outdoors could really help him.

Hart's Ridge Ranch offered a six-week program that

seemed to have it all. Experienced counselors, comfortable lodgings, gorgeous landscapes, and horses gentle enough to be ridden by autistic children. Best of all, it was reasonably affordable for her. Although she would've found a way to pay almost any price if it meant helping her son.

Looking out at the distant mountains, Tabitha admitted the program was for her as well. She felt like she hadn't had a break in years, and while she wouldn't trade any part of her life with Caden, she needed a change of pace.

Tabitha frowned. Caden's father, David Olsen, got plenty of breaks. He had bailed on them when Caden was two. He claimed he couldn't handle it.

Deep down, Tabitha had known her marriage wasn't going to work, even before Caden was born. She had married David at twenty-five, which seemed impossibly young now that she was in her thirties. Then she had gotten pregnant so soon after the wedding, and while she had been excited, she had also been nervous.

David hadn't been great at calming her down or being supportive. He had missed countless doctors' appointments, and he always had an excuse: work or friends or his family. But when Tabitha wanted to visit her family in Utah, David always found a reason not to.

When Caden was born and they found out he had autism, the lack of support from David only got worse. He seemed constantly disappointed in how his child had turned out, and that was one thing Tabitha could not bear.

After the divorce, she got full custody. David didn't even fight for partial custody. Now he had moved on with his life and only visited her and Caden once every few months.

When Tabitha saw the picture on Facebook a few months ago of David with his arm around his perfect fiancée, she had almost thrown her computer across the room. She and Caden were just David's messy first draft of a family. Well, that was fine. They didn't need or want him.

Tabitha tightened her grip on the steering wheel. She focused on the excitement of this next adventure and the rhythm of the country music humming from the radio. Caden had fussed and whined the first few hours of the road trip, unhappy with the music, but he had settled down once Tabitha found a country station. Country music and classical piano were Caden's favorite musical genres.

Caden had never ridden a horse, and Tabitha was a bit worried he might not like it. He could be very picky about his preferences. One of his aunts had sent him a pink pig stuffed animal for Christmas that year, and Caden had thrown a tantrum that still made Tabitha tremble to remember. He liked to collect blue pigs.

Experts didn't even like to call them "tantrums," but rather "behavioral seizures," and Tabitha felt that better described the way Caden would hurl himself on the ground or against a wall, wailing with an unmatched fervor. She feared the day he would get too big for her to wrap her arms around him and hold him until he calmed down and stopped flailing his arms.

Sophie, his occupational therapist, had assured Tabitha that Caden was actually developing very well, and both he and Tabitha would learn coping techniques as Caden got older. Even still, Tabitha worried about the future every single day. She knew from the blogs that worry was common among the parents of autistic children.

Tabitha glanced at the GPS. They were an hour away now.

If she were being honest, despite all that was exceptional about Hart's Ridge Ranch, they didn't have the best website. It was functional, but a bit out of date, and Tabitha's fingers had itched to give it a redesign. But she had not judged them by the website. She had read the backgrounds of all the occupational therapists and counselors who were going to be working at the program. Tabitha had been especially impressed by the certified instructors who would lead the horsemanship sessions. Caden and the other children in the program would learn everything about caring for and working with a horse.

Then there was the price. It was wildly discounted, a fraction of the price such programs usually were. As far as Tabitha could tell, Hart's Ridge Ranch was remarkably successful in horse training and breeding. This horsemanship program was just a passion project for Vera Hart, the matriarch of the family. She had also impressed Tabitha in the video calls they had shared. Vera was a true rancher; Tabitha could tell that right off the bat. The two of them had spent half of the first call discussing their shared experiences in ranch life. Then Vera explained that she had been working on setting up a program like the one for autistic children for over a decade. She wanted to do some good with her blessings, and now that her children were all grown up and helping with the ranch, she had more time and energy to pour into it.

Tabitha had been completely sold. She signed up for the six weeks after the first video call with Vera.

She had been looking forward to this trip for months, and now they were finally almost there.

Tabitha rolled down the window and let some of the fresh breeze blow through. It was still a bit chilly, but spring was on its way.

In his car seat, Caden blinked his eyes.

"Mommy." He let out a huge yawn. "Burger."

"Burger" meant food. Caden was verbal, but his communication and vocabulary skills weren't anywhere close to non-autistic children his age. Tabitha had long ago stopped comparing. Her only concern was Caden's happiness and well-being.

Tabitha smiled at him in the mirror. "Soon, sweetheart."

Caden pouted. Tabitha worried he might start to scream, but instead he turned to look out the window, staring fixedly at the rolling green pastures and the distant mountains.

"Horsies." He pointed at a field by the side of the highway. Tabitha had been showing him pictures and videos of farm animals for weeks to get him excited about this trip.

"Close." Tabitha laughed. "Those are cows, sweetheart. We'll see some horsies very soon."

Caden tilted his head and continued to stare, lost in thought.

Tabitha turned the knob on the radio up, ever so slightly. She knew playing it too loud would distress Caden.

Then she started to hum along to the song.

She was used to it being just her and Caden. She wouldn't have it any other way. And now she and her son were heading into their next adventure.

Tabitha only hoped her instincts had been right about the Hart family and their ranch.

CHAPTER 2

"All right, I think all the rooms are in good shape." Vera Hart put her hands on her hips and looked around the spacious living area of the large, new guesthouse.

"I agree." Isaac didn't point out to his mother that the place had been pristine for days. No one could possibly have prepared more for the start of the six-week horsemanship program than Vera.

He didn't hold it against his mother for her excitement. The ranch's newest venture meant a lot to her. She had first started researching horseback riding as autism therapy decades ago, and at last, the dream of hosting a program at Hart's Ridge Ranch was coming true.

Isaac hadn't minded helping with the administrative side. It kept him busy. He liked keeping busy. It spared him from spending too much time in his own head. Or reliving his past.

The program was starting small. Just four children and their parents. Vera insisted they had to start small in order to iron out any kinks and not take on more than they could handle.

The four visiting families were all staying in the large guesthouse on the property. It had four spacious, private family suites, a huge, shared kitchen and dining room, and a big living space for everyone to gather and relax after a long day at the ranch or watch movies on the large flat-screen TV. The guesthouse was also far enough from the main house that the families could feel as if they had some privacy from their hosts.

Not to mention the back porch boasted a stunning view of the Teton Range in the distance.

Each child had a bedroom that was attached or just next to their parents' bedroom, and Vera had stocked each guest suite with soaps and blankets that she had read were nonirritating to children with autism.

"The first day might be tough," Vera said. "Children on the spectrum can struggle when routines are disrupted, and obviously this is a big disruption."

"All of our counselors have the experience. You hired some great people, Mom." Isaac glanced down at the notepad in his hands, filled with the lists of tasks his mother had given him that morning. "Everything'll be fine."

He had moved all the furniture to where Vera had asked, and he had gone over the brochure and schedule pamphlets.

"If you don't need me for anything else, I ought to head back to work." It was high time he went back to his quiet office, where he preferred to spend his days.

His mother paused in her fretting as he started to exit the guesthouse.

"Actually, Isaac, would you mind staying to help me welcome everyone as they arrive and help transport luggage here?"

Isaac pressed his lips together. He had never been good at

saying no to her. He had always been happy to do whatever task, for the ranch, but his mother knew he didn't like being around people. Not anymore.

He wasn't exactly the social type—at least, not anymore. Not for a long time. He remembered brighter days, but he was a different man now. His domain was a solitary place, alone in his ranch office, taking care of the budget reports and the paperwork.

He glanced at his mother. "Wouldn't Jacob be a better greeter?"

"Jacob is busy with Elizabeth. Before you suggest Liam, he's teaching lessons all day. And you know Beau would never be able to focus enough for kids like these. He's a bit too high-energy himself, I think."

"Mateo?" Isaac hedged.

"Mateo is looking at horses with your dad."

Isaac frowned. He could have sworn he had more brothers, at least one who could help his mother out today, but Vera had listed all of them, except for Sawyer, who was traveling somewhere around the world, as usual, and hadn't returned to the ranch in years.

Isaac gave a reluctant nod. "All right, then."

He would stay and help, mainly because his mother had worked hard on this, but also because it was a good venture for the business, and he wanted it to be a success. The ranch was his only purpose anyway. It had been that way since he lost his wife. But he detested meeting strangers and having to make small talk. He wasn't going to be chipper; he no longer knew how. He knew his mother didn't expect that from him. When she wanted a Hart brother to be charming, she would rope in Liam or Beau.

There was a time, Isaac recalled as he followed his mother

on the walk through the woods back to the main house, when he would have been counted among the charming ones. He used to love to laugh and joke as much as Liam. He was once happy to stay up late chatting with people.

Not anymore. Now he found even the smallest amount of social interaction to be exhausting.

The loss of Anna and their child had reconfigured him. It was as if the grief had drained him dry of the essence of who he once was, and he had been filled back up with something more bitter and tired and bleak.

Isaac stood behind Vera and the counselors who'd been hired for the six weeks. They were all staying in another pair of guesthouses on the ranch, one for the women and one for the men. Vera and Tom had been building extra structures and renovating existing ones ever since they began expanding the ranch over thirty-five years ago. Vera joked that she wanted to build a few big houses for her sons and their growing families too, a not-so-subtle hint that she was eager for lots of grandchildren.

She never told that joke in front of Isaac, but he'd heard it enough from his brothers. Sometimes he really believed he would have preferred everyone to just treat him the same as they had before. As much as he appreciated his family's care and consideration, when they tiptoed around him and certain topics, it made Isaac feel even more conscious of everything he'd lost.

In any case, Vera and Tom would likely get their grandchildren soon. Jacob and Elizabeth were preparing for their wedding, and Beau and Liam likely weren't far behind, as both of them were smitten with their girlfriends, Diane and Lily, respectively. Mateo had just gotten engaged to Claire and given the fact that he had been yearning for her for ten years,

Isaac figured they wouldn't waste much time heading for the altar.

He was happy for all of them. He wouldn't begrudge his brothers a fraction of their happiness. And he hoped they never knew what it was like when that kind of happiness and love was ripped away.

Isaac shoved his hands in his pockets as his mother chatted with Donna Jones, the certified instructor who would be leading all the activities. Donna had previously worked with several similar programs and was visibly thrilled to be at Hart's Ridge Ranch.

In the distance, a car appeared.

Vera's eyes lit up as she spotted it. The first family was arriving. "Here they come!"

There were four families enrolled in the program. A couple from New York with a ten-year-old, and another couple from Indiana with an eight-year-old. Then a mother was coming solo with her six-year-old daughter as her husband would remain in Texas working. The fourth was a single mother from California with a six-year-old son. Vera had gushed about all of them, but she seemed especially fond of the single mother.

Isaac couldn't even imagine being a single parent, much less one with a child with special needs. He wondered if this woman had lost her husband to death or divorce. Maybe she'd never married at all. Regardless, it was none of his business, and he had no intention of asking. His job was to act like a normal human being and help welcome everyone, then haul their luggage out to the guesthouse. He was already counting the seconds before he could escape back to his office.

The first car held the woman from Texas, Cindy, and her

daughter, Daisy. The girl was tired from the journey, but she looked around with bright, curious eyes.

Isaac and another counselor carried their luggage to the guesthouse while Vera and Donna showed Cindy and Daisy around. By the time Isaac returned, the couple from Indiana was arriving, shortly followed by the couple from New York.

Their children, Ben and Tessa, had both done similar programs and seemed relatively at ease as they sized each other up. Daisy was withdrawn, drinking an apple juice and warily watching the surrounding people.

All the families had headed to the guesthouse when the final attendee arrived in the driveway.

"This must be Tabitha Young and Caden," Vera said, smiling as the car pulled to a stop.

Isaac was silently grateful he only had one last bit of luggage to transport.

The car door opened and closed while Isaac squinted into the distance.

He heard his mother greet the newcomer, and he heard a murmured reply.

Then he looked the woman full in the face.

She was beautiful. Isaac didn't know what he had been picturing for a single mother, but it wasn't the raven-haired beauty with eyes that seemed to take up half her sweet, elfin face.

She was young, too. As Tabitha reached into the back seat to unbuckle her son from his car seat, Isaac wondered how old she was. She couldn't be much more than thirty. Perhaps around his own age.

She looked too young to be taking care of her son all alone, that was for sure. Isaac felt a brief and powerful surge of hatred for whoever had left this woman alone. And yet that hatred was tempered by a bizarre relief that she wasn't taken. She was single.

Isaac shook his head and stepped forward. He would carry the luggage and then get far away from this woman.

But just then her son let out a yell. Tabitha lifted him out of the car, but he began shrieking and flailing his arms.

Tabitha's mouth pressed into a thin line as she wrapped her arms around her son's chest and started murmuring in his ear.

Isaac felt a pang of sympathy as he realized she was embarrassed. She had no reason for it. Everyone here understood.

He figured she had probably lived through this scene dozens of times. At the grocery store. At the park. He couldn't imagine how strong she had to be to get used to the stares and the judgment from people who were unaware or simply misunderstood her child.

"Caden, breathe. I'm here, okay?" Tabitha looked up at Vera and Donna, her cheeks stained red. "I'm so sorry about this."

"It's fine." Donna gave her a reassuring smile. "And, of course, understandable after such a long drive and in a new environment."

Vera opened her mouth to echo Donna, but her words were cut off when Caden let out a howl and thrashed so hard that Tabitha lost her grip on him. Caden's eyes were squeezed shut as he fought his mother's hold, and Isaac couldn't stop himself from stepping forward in concern. The boy was going to plummet to the ground.

Isaac knew he wasn't trained. He had no idea how to handle this kind of behavior. And he knew he had no business touching someone else's child. Yet his hands moved to gently grip Caden's small shoulders, and by some miracle, the touch seemed to dampen the boy's tantrum.

Caden went perfectly still as he opened his eyes and tipped his neck back to look up at Isaac.

The red flush left his face as he inhaled. His cheeks were damp from his tears.

Isaac knew he could be an intimidating sight, especially to a child. He was tall and dark-eyed, and usually wore a somber expression beneath his large black hat. He attempted to give the boy a reassuring smile.

Caden cocked his small head as he took in a deep breath. "Woody?"

Isaac glanced up in question at Tabitha, who stood just behind her son, her brow creased with worry. Before he could say anything, Caden spoke up again.

"Cowboy." He pointed at Isaac, and to everyone's collective relief, his face was lit up with a bright smile. "Woody."

"Woody from Toy Story." On a small, relieved-sounding laugh, Tabitha stepped forward, placing a gentle hand on her son's back. She was so close Isaac caught the scent of her long hair and a warm sweetness that pulled at him from somewhere deep down. He was once again struck by her beauty as she offered him a shy smile. "It's one of Caden's favorite movies."

Isaac nodded once in acknowledgment. He didn't know what possessed him, but all he knew was that he wanted to make this small child and his mother happy.

He leaned down toward Caden and said, in a serious tone, "There's a snake in my boot."

Caden let out a shriek of laughter and jumped up and down, clapping his hands. He whirled to his mother and grabbed her hand, excited words spilling out of him about cowboys and horses and Toy Story.

Tabitha nodded along, and then she looked up at Isaac and smiled—really smiled.

The sight of her radiant grin nearly undid him.

Tabitha Young was a beautiful, kind woman; any man with a pair of functioning eyes could see that. But when she smiled, she was absolutely stunning.

CHAPTER 3

Tabitha had wanted a hole to open up in the ground when Caden had started wailing as soon as they arrived.

She knew it was absurd to be embarrassed, but she had wanted to at least make a good first impression. It was silly to worry, she knew. If there was ever a place where Caden wouldn't be judged, it was at a program specifically designed for children with autism.

Even so, Tabitha didn't enjoy looking like she had no control over her child. She knew she could always weather a tantrum of Caden's, but she also knew the scenes were jarring to those unused to them. She had seen the discomfort in a stranger's eyes when Caden had an episode at the grocery store. She had even felt the unease of her own family when Caden started shrieking during a holiday supper. People didn't know how to react. And they pitied her. After so many years, Tabitha was used to that.

When Caden had jerked out of her grasp, and the tall, dark-haired cowboy stepped forward, Tabitha had stiffened.

The stoic, handsome man didn't seem like a counselor, or at least he hadn't been mentioned in the comprehensive report of all the program staff Tabitha had read about before signing up. Whoever he was, Tabitha generally didn't like other people trying to calm down her son. It rarely ended well.

But then a miracle had occurred. The cowboy touched Caden's shoulders, and while Caden usually hated when strangers touched him, he had instead relaxed, his fascination with the cowboy taking over.

And when the kind man had indulged Caden by quoting *Toy Story*, Tabitha could have thrown her arms around his neck and hugged him, she was that grateful.

She realized now she was still smiling up at him. "Thank you."

He nodded politely and stepped back, and then Vera Hart was at Tabitha's side.

"Tabitha, this is my son Isaac." Vera beamed up at her attractive son, who towered head and shoulders over her. "He's been helping out with the organization of this program."

"Ma'am." Isaac tipped the brim of his hat but said nothing more. Then he turned to pick up her and Caden's luggage.

"I'll show you to where you'll be staying," Vera said. She gestured toward a path that led behind the large ranch house. Isaac followed behind them, carrying the bags. "We'll get you settled," Vera said, "then we'll have supper in a few hours."

"Thank you. That sounds great." Tabitha held on to Caden's hand and looked out at the sprawling lands and the mountain range in the distance. "Your family's ranch is beautiful."

The pastures were lined with fences that were in good repair, and the huge stables looked clean and well-maintained. Tabitha had spent enough of her childhood on ranches that she had a good eye. She could tell when a ranch was flourishing and when it was struggling, and Hart's Ridge Ranch was definitely flourishing.

The horses in the nearest pasture were gleaming with health. Tabitha wasn't much of an expert when it came to the details of a horse's pedigree, but she sensed that these animals were the pinnacle in good breeding.

Caden stopped to point at the animals, and Tabitha's heart leapt at his excitement. Aside from his outburst when they first arrived, his grin hadn't dimmed for a moment. This had been the right choice, bringing him here.

When they paused, Isaac drew up next to them.

Caden let go of Tabitha's hand to step closer to his new favorite person. Tabitha had never seen her son gravitate toward a stranger so quickly.

"Horsies!" Caden shouted. "Horsies!"

"Yes, we've got plenty of those around here." Where Isaac didn't seem to have more than two words for Tabitha, he spoke easily and patiently to Caden. Not in a forced way, like some people did, but in a normal tone that warmed Tabitha's heart. So many people thought autistic children didn't know when they were being treated differently, but in her experience, Caden and other children like him were very intuitive. They couldn't read certain communicative cues, but they still sensed shifting energies. They knew when someone was inherently kind, like Isaac Hart.

Tabitha watched him, feeling a flutter in her stomach. He was tall and lean, but strong in the way ranchers always were from working the land and riding long hours in the saddle. There was a quiet strength to him, and the way he moved was almost graceful. He was clean-shaven, and his face was surprisingly fine boned, with sharp cheekbones and a strong jaw. His warm, dark eyes were the color of melted chocolate, but she couldn't help noticing that his kind smiles never quite seemed to reach them.

Tabitha was surprised by the sudden flutter of nerves she felt as she stole glances at Isaac out of the corner of her eye. As a teenager, she had her share of fleeting crushes on cowboys. Something about their plaid shirts, wide-brimmed hats, and rugged boots made her feel like a schoolgirl again, heading out for a rare Friday night date or to watch football games. Back then, she had been so lighthearted about life, so much younger and freer.

She was a different person now, and after she'd moved to California for school and then work, she hadn't come across very many cowboys in her day-to-day life.

As for Isaac Hart, Tabitha hadn't felt this kind of instant attraction for a man in years. The divorce had left her in no mind for dating, and then she had been so busy with work and raising Caden that even the idea of meeting someone new left her exhausted.

Tabitha swung her attention back to her son and quickened her pace as Caden set off ahead of everyone and began to meander across the huge green lawn. She didn't want him wandering too far off on his own.

Caden had to be her sole focus. And he was. She wouldn't trade life with her son for the world, and she had no regrets about how things had turned out. She loved Caden too much for that.

She definitely hadn't come to the program at Hart's Ridge Ranch looking for romance. Who would want to date a stressed-out, perpetually drained single mother, anyway? Especially one who would never hesitate to cancel plans and prioritize her son.

Not any man she had ever run across, that was for sure. Tabitha wasn't bitter, nor did she hold her own loneliness against Caden. She had always been independent. When she realized her marriage was over, she simply told herself she would have to do it alone. She knew she could. For Caden, she would do anything.

But as Vera continued ahead of them now and Isaac fell into step beside Tabitha, she found herself wanting to strike up a conversation. It couldn't hurt to get to know him a little. After all, she was here for six weeks; she might as well make a few friends.

"Thank you again for earlier, Isaac. For being kind to my son."

He shook his head. "No need to thank me. It was nothing."

"No, it wasn't." Tabitha nodded toward Caden, who was still transfixed on the horses in the pasture. "You were really good with him. He likes you."

"Well, I have a bunch of younger brothers," Isaac said, his deep voice calm and reflective. "I'm used to handling a bit of chaos."

It was generous of Isaac to compare Caden to his own younger brothers. She knew none of Vera and Tom Hart's sons were on the spectrum. During one of their many chats, Vera had mentioned that she didn't have any close relatives with autism, but she had learned about horsemanship as therapy years ago and been taken with the concept ever since.

"Are you the oldest?" Tabitha asked.

"No, that's my brother Jacob. I'm the second," Isaac said. "There are four younger than us."

"Big family," Tabitha said. "I can relate. I've got four sisters; we all grew up on a ranch in Utah."

"You see them often?" Isaac asked.

"No." Tabitha shook her head. "I've been in San Francisco for years, and with Caden, I don't travel much. Coming here is a real treat—for me, as much as for him."

"Well, once a ranch girl, always a ranch girl." Isaac's smile was fleeting, almost as if he didn't use it very often.

Tabitha laughed and agreed. She heard the warm tone in her own voice. She hadn't put this much effort into chatting with a man in a very long time. She wasn't flirting, but there was something about Isaac that made her wish she was better at making small talk. As they walked together, side by side, she felt her step lighten, her heart beating a little faster.

As the guesthouse came into view, part of her wanted to slow her pace if only so she could spend more time getting to know him.

She wondered if he felt it, too.

CHAPTER 4

Isaac's boots crunched on the gravel as he headed toward the guesthouse with Tabitha.

His attraction to her was unexpected, and he didn't like how it made him feel. Like he was betraying Anna simply by talking with another woman. It had been three years, but when would it ever be long enough for his heart?

He had loved Anna deeply, with everything he had, and losing her and their baby had shattered him in ways he thought he might never heal. He still felt the cracks every day, the places where the pain seeped through like water from a broken dam. But today, with Tabitha, something had shifted, and he wasn't sure how to handle it.

He hadn't felt this alive, this engaged in something other than his work, in a long time. It wasn't just Tabitha's beauty, though she certainly had that in spades. It was the way she had handled her son, Caden, with such patience and love. He admired that. He admired her obvious inner strength, too. He felt drawn to it.

He felt drawn to her.

That realization was enough to give him the urge to bolt. He couldn't let himself get caught up in some silly infatuation, least of all with a guest at the ranch. Casual relationships had never been his thing, and aside from that, he never mixed ranch business with personal.

The ranch was his lifeline, his anchor in the storm that had become his life. It was the one thing that had helped him survive after losing Anna and the baby. He was determined not to let anything, or anyone, distract him from that.

Not even a beautiful single mother with wide, caring eyes and a wholesome kindness that radiated from her like sunshine.

He was relieved when they reached the guesthouse. His mother sailed in ahead of them to greet the other families who'd already settled in. Isaac stepped away to put Tabitha and Caden's bags in their assigned suite. The hubbub of excited voices drifted in from the huge living area as Tabitha and Caden were swept away into the gathering of the other guests and introductions were made.

Isaac lingered for a moment in the quiet of Tabitha's suite, his head a jumble and his emotions caught in a conflicted tangle. Being around other families brought a wave of grief that he struggled to hold at bay. It was hard not to think about what he'd lost. Anna. Their baby girl.

Alice. That's what he had named the tiny baby girl. His mother was the one who had gently reminded him, in those wretched days after the long night at the hospital when he was making arrangements for not one headstone, but two, that his precious daughter needed a name.

Isaac shouldn't have been the one choosing. He and Anna should have done that together.

They had discussed options, and they had picked out their

favorite names for a boy and a girl, but he and Anna wanted to make the final decision once they met their child.

Isaac never thought he would have to choose the name alone.

He named her Alice, inspired by one of Anna's favorite books, *Alice in Wonderland.* It was a name that felt full of possibility and life, even though his daughter had never had the chance to experience any of it. Naming her had been the hardest decision he'd ever made, but it had also been a way to honor the love he and Anna shared. He hoped she would approve.

Isaac's jaw tightened. How could he ever let go of the past when that's where Anna and Alice existed?

His heart didn't have room for anything but their memory and the pain of their loss.

And yet, something about Tabitha made him curious, made him want to know more about her. That was a new feeling for him. And a confusing one.

He stepped out to the living area, his gaze homing in on Tabitha no matter how he wanted to avoid her. Crossing his arms, he leaned against the wall and forced himself to focus on his mother and Donna as they gave a brief welcome speech, then started to hand out the schedule for the next few days.

Tabitha sat on a couch with Caden next to her and the little girl Daisy on her other side. She bent over the schedule, reading it with care. Isaac stared at the way her long, dark hair fell in smooth waves over her shoulders and down her back.

"All right, I'll let you all get settled in here," Vera said. "And once again, I am so honored and happy to have you here for our inaugural program."

Everyone clapped, and then the group dispersed.

Isaac should have left too, but for some reason, his boots remained planted where he stood, until Tabitha glanced his way and made eye contact with him. She got up and walked toward him, holding Caden's hand.

Isaac cleared his throat. "I can show you to your room," he said. "I already put your luggage in."

"That would be great, thanks." Tabitha looked down at Caden. "Let's go see where we're staying, hon."

The way she interacted with her son, the loving way she looked at the boy, made a lump rise in Isaac's throat.

He turned away and quickly led them to their guest suite with its two adjoining bedrooms.

Caden stood outside the threshold to his room and stared with a dubious eye.

"Oh, look, there are trucks on your bedsheets. Isn't that nice?" Tabitha stepped inside and patted the small bed. "We can put all your stuffed animals right here, okay?"

"No." Caden shook his head. "I want my room."

Tabitha sat down on the bed and held his gaze. "This is your room, sweetheart. It's just a bit different."

Caden seemed worried, so Isaac spoke up. "This here is a cowboy room."

Caden was instantly alert. "Cowboy?"

Tabitha cast Isaac a grateful look. "Exactly. See, there's even a cowboy hat for you."

Caden moved to the little desk his mother pointed at and picked up the hat that had been left for him. He inspected every inch of it, then awkwardly set it on top of his head.

Tabitha nodded her approval. "Looks great, kiddo."

She stood up and crossed the room, so close to Isaac that he held his breath.

"You're like magic with him," Tabitha said. "Did you take a course like your mom?"

"No." Isaac stepped backward, already inching toward the door. "I'm just helping out where I can."

She smiled that devastating smile again, part gratitude, and something else he didn't want to analyze. "Maybe I'll see you around at some of the kids' activities?"

He quickly shook his head. "No, ma'am. Probably not. My work generally keeps me busy in my office out at the stables."

"Oh." Was it disappointment he heard in her voice? She probably was hoping he'd be a handy distraction for Caden when she needed him.

At any rate, he had lingered too long. "Speaking of work, I should get back to it."

She gave him a slight smile. "Of course. It was really nice meeting you, Isaac."

"Ma'am," he murmured, hoping his clipped tone didn't come off as gruff as it sounded to his own ears. Tipping his hat, he pivoted and strode for the door before Tabitha's smiles or her sweet, heavenly scent had a chance to addle him any more than it already had.

Once outside, he exhaled deeply, a breath that felt like it had been pent up inside him for years. He wasn't ready to admit to anything more than curiosity where Tabitha was concerned, but today was only the first day. How was he going to get through the next six weeks without running into her or Caden?

Somehow, he'd manage. For now, he needed to keep his focus where it belonged—on the ranch. That was what mattered. That was what kept him going.

Isaac straightened up, rolling his shoulders back as he began walking, his stride purposeful. There were a hundred things that needed doing, and he was determined to not let his mind wander back to thoughts of the intriguing, raven-haired woman with the soft voice and the bright, resilient smile. He would stay busy, keep his hands and mind occupied, and not let his heart get involved with Tabitha or her little boy.

Isaac reached the stables and felt the familiar calm settle over him as he paused outside the wide doors. This was his place, his sanctuary. He had work to do, and that was where he'd find his peace. Isaac resolved to keep his mind on the ranch and his responsibilities, not on things he couldn't have —or shouldn't want.

He glanced back toward the guesthouse one last time, then shook his head and went inside, ready to drown his thoughts in the steady, comforting rhythm of work.

CHAPTER 5

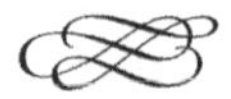

By suppertime, Tabitha was feeling well-rested and energetic.

She had also recovered from Isaac's somewhat abrupt exit.

She understood it. Being around children with autism could be uncomfortable for people not accustomed to it. As kind as he'd been, Isaac no doubt had reached his limit with her and Caden. Similar things had happened before, so it wasn't as if Tabitha hadn't been prepared for Isaac to hurry away to somewhere else. So, it really shouldn't have stung as much as it did.

Tabitha pushed the thought from her mind as she led Caden up to the ranch's main house for the first supper of their stay.

By her side was Cindy, another parent in the program. Cindy was married, but she was also alone since her husband had to remain in Texas for his job.

The two women had fallen into an easy camaraderie. Cindy's daughter Daisy was close to Caden in age, and Cindy and Tabitha had already talked for a while about their shared experiences and their hopes for the program.

"Have you read that parenting blog by the mom in Australia?" Cindy asked as they crossed the wide lawn toward the house.

Tabitha nodded enthusiastically. "Yes, I love that one. I've actually direct messaged her a few times on her socials. She's great, and so helpful."

Cindy started to rattle off more favorite blogs they had in common as they entered the main house. Being with another parent of a child on the spectrum was hugely comforting, like finding someone in a foreign country who spoke your native language.

Cindy was a few years older than Tabitha and had two other children, who were both neurotypical. Tabitha couldn't imagine what it was like to have to juggle so much.

"You get used to it." Cindy sighed. "But also, I don't sleep anymore."

Tabitha chuckled as they entered a large dining room, which had a long wooden table at its center and another one situated along the far wall and laden with large serving bowls and platters full of delicious-smelling food.

Vera Hart stood near the buffet, a big smile on her face as all her guests arrived for the meal. A handsome, dark-haired man with kind brown eyes stood beside her.

"Welcome, everyone. Come in and make yourselves comfortable." Vera gestured at the food. "My son Mateo and I just finished setting everything out for supper. Help yourself while it's hot."

The table looked like a cornucopia, and it was all comfort food. There was fried chicken, mashed potatoes, a mixed-greens salad, and a huge pot of macaroni and cheese. Vera had taken the time to collect all the dietary preferences and food allergies of the children and adults on their applications, which meant a lot to Tabitha. Caden could be a picky eater, and she knew he wasn't the only child in the room to be that way.

While Cindy and Tabitha served their children and themselves, another two men walked in. Vera introduced the older, gray-haired one as her husband, Tom, and the younger one with the wild gleam in his eyes as her son Beau, adding that he mostly worked at the ranch training new horses.

Cindy leaned close to Tabitha as they sat down. "These Hart sons certainly are easy on the eyes, aren't they?"

Tabitha giggled as she cut up Caden's food.

She glanced up at Mateo and Beau. They were attractive men, for sure, but in her opinion, Isaac was the best-looking one. There was something so intriguing in his kind, yet haunted, eyes, something appealing in his quiet, yet capable, way of moving. She had only just met him, but even so, he made her feel at peace—even while he made her heartbeat race a bit faster.

He finally arrived just after the last of the other parents had entered the dining room. Taking the vacant seat to the right of Tom Hart at the far end of the table, Isaac barely gave Tabitha a glance as he and the rest of the gathered group settled in for supper. They all sat around the huge table with the entire Hart family. It felt like a huge family supper, and everyone fell into excited conversation about the days ahead in the program.

Liam was the brother who talked the most, and he seemed totally at ease with the children. Vera had mentioned that he taught most of the horsemanship lessons at the stables, including working with children, but dealing with little ones like Caden, Daisy, and the others presented additional challenges and required extra patience. Even so, Liam didn't miss a beat as he chatted with Luke, the oldest child in the program.

Tabitha eavesdropped on the conversation. She was impressed by Luke and was dying to pick his parents' brains for advice. Luke was verbal and had a sunny personality that was plain for all to see. He clearly had his unique needs—his shirt was buttoned all the way up just so, his hair was perfectly combed, and his clothes were all meticulously color-coordinated. If Caden grew up to be as bright and happy as Luke, Tabitha would be thrilled.

The fourth child was Molly, a quiet eight-year-old. Tabitha recalled from the exchange of emails before the program that her parents, Jessica and Mike, were from Indiana. Molly stuck close to her mother's side and definitely was similar to Caden in that she wasn't generally at ease around strangers.

Between listening to the others and making sure Caden was okay, Tabitha sneaked a few glances at Isaac.

Despite the company and lively conversation of all the family members and their significant others, Isaac was a solitary presence at the table. Reserved and quiet, he listened politely to the chatter circulating the group, but added nothing of his own. It hadn't gone unnoticed by Tabitha that he was the only one without a girlfriend or fiancée. For most of the meal, he kept his head down and only spoke occasionally to his father seated beside him.

His mother and brothers, meanwhile, chatted nonstop. Liam flirted with his girlfriend, Lily, who sported a sardonic smile and rolled her eyes at him often. Even so, it was clear she adored him. Equally smitten was Beau. His elegant girlfriend, Diane, also trained horses at the ranch, according to

Vera. Tabitha was quite sure she had never seen a better-looking couple than blue-eyed Beau and blonde Diane. Mateo Hart was almost as quiet as Isaac, but only because he was basking in the effervescence of his bubbly girlfriend, Claire, who eschewed the ranch dress code of blue jeans and button-down shirts for a stylish plaid minidress and cozy cardigan.

Tabitha knew she shouldn't have felt such a thrill at the discovery that Isaac was single.

She wondered why. He was almost as old as his older brother Jacob, who seemed head over heels in love with his fiancée, Elizabeth. And Tabitha was certain there were plenty of women who would love to hitch their wagons to Isaac's, so to speak.

As soon as the meal was over, Isaac rose and started to help clear the plates. Tabitha found herself hoping he would linger at the table, but he disappeared into the kitchen and didn't come back.

She shrugged off his remote demeanor and focused instead on Caden. He was the reason she was here, after all. She certainly hadn't driven all the way to Wyoming to crush on a handsome, obviously uninterested cowboy.

After supper Donna and the counselors, along with Vera, all sat in the living room and gave extended introductions.

Caden was glued to Tabitha's side, which was pretty standard when he was around strangers.

Tabitha felt a bit shy as well, but when Veronica, a mom from New York, turned to her and asked if she was the same Tabitha Young who wrote a guest post on a popular autism blogger's site, Tabitha could only smile.

"Yes, that was me," she admitted, completely surprised. "You actually read my post?"

"It was so good," Veronica enthused. "You write with the perfect blend of humor and heart."

"Maybe you should start your own blog." Veronica's husband, Hunter, leaned forward as he made the suggestion. "Seriously, that post was a big hit with my wife and her friends back in New York."

"Thank you." Tabitha's cheeks flushed from the praise. She had to admit, she had thought about writing before. With her experience in web design, she knew she could create a useful site for those who wanted to know more about raising a child with autism. Between caring for Caden and her own job, she just never seemed to have enough time to take on anything new.

As the supper gathering ended and the group of parents walked back to the guesthouse, Tabitha mused that maybe if this program went well, she could try writing a few posts about her experience and see what happened. She could also get some awesome photos of the ranch while she was here.

Caden was exhausted by the time they got back to their bunk rooms. Tabitha decided it was a good thing he was worn out. He usually got upset by changes to his routine, but the fact that he was so tired might make it easier for him to fall asleep.

During bath time, she told him all about the horses he was going to meet tomorrow. Then she helped him into a pair of pajamas that featured little cars on the pants and top. She had a matching set for herself, which she'd special ordered at Caden's insistence. She felt silly wearing them, but it made her son smile, and that was more than worth it.

She and Caden spent half an hour setting up his stuffed animals just so in his temporary room, and Tabitha breathed a sigh of relief that Caden didn't seem too upset by the new setting.

Years before, they had visited her parents in Utah, and Caden had screamed for an entire night because the windows in the room weren't right. The fact that he was taking this totally new bedroom and living arrangement in stride warmed Tabitha's heart.

She sat by his bed until he fell into a deep sleep. Then she sat a while longer, enjoying the sound of his breathing.

He lay on his back, with his arms thrown up on either side of his head. It was nearly impossible to resist snuggling in beside him, but the last thing she wanted was to wake him up.

Instead, she simply watched her little boy sleep, gratified by the look of utter peace on his angelic face.

When Tabitha finally went to bed herself, she felt more content than she had in a long while. She knew in her heart she had made the right choice bringing Caden to this place.

CHAPTER 6

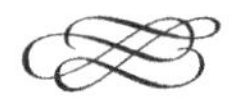

Isaac woke at five as he did every day, and within an hour, he was in his office with the door shut.

Usually, if he wasn't disturbed, he could get in several hours of work in the morning. There was always plenty to do in the office. The ranch was so large and had so many different moving parts, there was no end to the payrolls and the bills of sale and the emails to be sent, not to mention the scheduling of the stalls that were rented out.

Isaac had always been good at focusing. He never struggled with schoolwork, like Beau and Liam occasionally did. And after Anna died, Isaac only found relief when he was buried in paperwork and other business tasks.

It was the only time the pain went away. When he shut off all his emotions and focused on balancing the books.

He knew his family members thought it was a bad way of coping. Every few months for the past year, Jacob would try to get Isaac to take on horse training or lessons, anything that got him out of the office. Liam would constantly invite Isaac out to bars or parties, and Beau had badgered him about attending more rodeos. His mother had even suggested therapy, which Isaac had attempted for a few months but eventually stopped going. He appreciated everyone's help and concern, but nothing was going to pull him out of his grief until he was ready to let it go.

For now, he was coping in the only way he knew how. Prayer had helped some. Steady work had helped. Time would have to do the rest. Even then, Isaac had his doubts.

Every time he engaged with other people, he was reminded of the family he had wanted so badly and lost. Teaching riding lessons to children only reminded him of the child he had to bury. Riding horses every day only reminded him of the long rides he used to take with Anna, her hair streaming out from beneath her hat and her laughter carrying on the wind.

His family wanted him to participate in life. They thought that would heal him. What they didn't understand was that participating in life only made his wounds deeper.

So, his piles of paperwork weren't holding him back from healing as his mom sometimes suggested. It was holding him together.

That morning, though, Isaac couldn't focus on his work.

He had gone over the schedule so often with his mother that he knew exactly what the kids and their parents were doing at every hour.

At nine, they were meeting for breakfast. Then they would have a session with one of the counselors and Donna to explore the ranch and get used to the environment.

They wouldn't meet the horses until the afternoon. According to Donna, it was always better to go slow. First, get the kids used to the new setting. Then introduce them to horses, but no riding until all the children were used to being around the horses.

In the past few weeks, Isaac had picked up more than he ever thought he would about horseback riding as autism therapy. Apparently, some children on the spectrum found it easier to have an emotional and intuitive connection with horses than with other people. Working with horses helped these children identify and express emotions. It even improved their communication. Vera had shown him study after study that showed how working with horses had huge results when it came to children's classroom performance as well as verbal and nonverbal communication skills.

It was interesting to Isaac that the studies confirmed something he and his family had always known instinctively. Horses were very empathetic animals. They felt what their riders felt, and vice versa. It was one of the first lessons his father had taught all of them when they'd started riding: if you were scared, your horse would be scared. If you were happy, your horse would be happy.

So, of course, that empathy and connection could be experienced between a horse and a child with autism.

By midmorning, Isaac had accomplished only half of what he usually did. The office had no windows, except for a tiny square that let in a beam of light and offered a view of a small sliver of the pasture.

He kept glancing at the door, almost wishing someone would burst in and disturb his peace.

Usually, he resented interruptions. He always got annoyed as the day wore on, and the stables got busier. Most afternoons, there were so many people wandering in and out of the office that Isaac sometimes took himself off on a long walk. Sometimes a ride. He still rode, but much less than he once had.

He could never stop, though. Riding was like breathing to him, and he knew his brothers felt the same.

Isaac purposely waited until two in the afternoon before he headed up to the main house to grab a quick bite to eat. He was starving, but he knew the program was having their lunch from noon to one o'clock, and he wanted to miss them.

He didn't want to dwell on why he was avoiding the program members.

Her name was Tabitha Young.

It had been nearly impossible for him to keep his eyes off Tabitha during supper the night before. She had sat there at the table, radiant and smiling, and every fiber of Isaac's being had yearned to sit next to her. To ask her questions. To find out about her life. To make her laugh.

So, he had forced himself to sit as far away as possible and keep his head down. He hadn't spoken much, but his family was certainly used to that. None of them had noticed his penchant for Tabitha. And they never would.

It was a bad idea to get near her. He wasn't ready for a relationship, much less a relationship with a single mother. He was never going to be ready for that kind of risk again. When you shared a life with someone, that entire existence could be ruined in a matter of hours. Isaac couldn't stomach that. Not again.

So he crept into his own family's kitchen like some sort of thief, dreading that he would round a corner and find Tabitha there.

Of course, the kitchen was empty. All the kids and parents were out at the pasture, meeting the horses.

His family had spent months finding and training the ideal horses for the program. The horses had to have calm temperaments, as well as be used to children and other animals. They also had to be gentle and easy to ride. Isaac felt they were prepared, with six horses that he was confident were ideal. A few of the horses Liam used with the youngest children who took lessons, and some of them had been trained specifically to work with children and adults on the spectrum.

Of course, there were some horses on the ranch that Isaac wouldn't want any child or inexperienced adult to get within fifty yards of. The horses they acquired for breeding tended to be high-spirited and easily bucked or spooked. And then there were the untrained horses that Beau and Diane worked with. The ranch had just purchased a stallion named Jester, and a gorgeous but easily spooked mare called Maeve. They were beautiful and majestic animals, and Beau couldn't stop talking about them, but they balked at loud noises. Jester had already tossed anyone who tried to get on his back, and Maeve had clipped a trainer who approached her too suddenly the other day by kicking out her back hooves.

Vera and Donna had dedicated a lot of time and energy into making sure those horses were separated from the program. Every single ranch employee had undergone special training on this.

After Isaac ate his sandwich, he figured he might as well stretch his legs. He could endure office work far longer than any of his brothers, but he still had a limit. He needed to spend a bit of time outdoors each day.

He exited the ranch house, and his feet took him left, to where the kids were meeting with the horses in the paddock. He could have turned right and watched Liam teach a lesson, or he could have walked the half mile to the training pen where Beau and Diane were. But instead, he turned left.

Isaac told himself it was only natural curiosity. The program was brand new, and he wanted to see how it was going. For business reasons.

He halted a good twenty yards from the pasture, up on the hillside, overlooking it.

From the look on his mother's face, where she was standing in the center of the pasture, the first full day was going well.

The oldest student, Luke, was grinning up at a horse and already petting the soft nose. The older girl, Molly, was standing a bit away from her assigned horse, but she was peppering the counselor nearby with questions.

Daisy and Caden, the two youngest members of the program, stood side by side, observing the horses from a distance and wearing matching helmets. Isaac's heart seemed to throb as he noted how adorable they looked.

Then he spotted Tabitha, and he couldn't look anywhere else.

She was standing by one of the horses, her hand stroking its neck, as she turned toward her son and smiled. She said something, and Isaac imagined she was telling Caden how sweet the horse was.

Tabitha was wearing worn cowboy boots and durable jeans with a button-down shirt. She looked totally at ease around the horses. She had told him she grew up in a ranching area of Utah, but even so, Isaac was surprised at just how well she fit in with the horses.

He had an uncontrollable urge to see her ride. To watch her mount a horse and kick it into a gallop.

Tabitha stepped away as the counselor named Ben, who

had flown in from a similar program in Montana, led Caden by the hand toward the horse.

Tabitha retreated to the edge of the fence. She kept one eye on her son, but she was clearly willing to let the counselors do their job. Part of the program was about teaching independence and responsibility.

Isaac was moving toward her before he even knew what he was doing. It was as if some instinct called him to go to her side as soon as she was on her own.

She looked over her shoulder as he approached, and her mouth broke into a wide smile.

"Good afternoon." Tabitha grabbed the fence and climbed over in a few graceful movements.

Then she was standing on the other side, next to Isaac.

"It looks like it's going well." He nodded toward the children and horses.

Tabitha's hair was pulled back, and her face glowed with pleasure. "It really is. Caden is loving it so far."

Isaac nodded and looked away. He was aware that he was being unimaginably awkward, but it was sinking in that he had vowed to stay away from Tabitha that day, yet here he was, already drawn to her within an hour of leaving his office.

Clearly, his office would be the only safe space over the next few weeks.

He had never felt drawn to a woman like this. Not since Anna.

Isaac turned away from Tabitha, unable to look at her. He felt like a traitor. It was inherently wrong for him to feel this way about anyone other than Anna. Wasn't it?

He had never thought about betraying Anna because he had never thought he would want to.

Now, for the first time, it was becoming a distinct possibility.

Isaac took a deep breath and turned back toward Tabitha, forcing himself to meet her eyes. Her gaze was calm, inviting. He was surprised at how easy it was to talk to her, even with all the turmoil churning inside him.

"I have to admit," he began, keeping his tone light, "I was a bit skeptical about this whole program at first. But seeing Caden and the others out there... It seems like it might actually be doing some good."

Tabitha's smile grew, and he felt a warmth spread through his chest at the sight. "I think so," she replied softly. "Caden's had a hard time with new environments, but he's really taken to this place. I wasn't sure if he'd even get this close to a horse on the first day, but he's already so curious."

Isaac nodded, glancing out toward the paddock where the children were gathered. "It's a good thing," he said. "Horses have a way of calming people down. They're intuitive like that."

Tabitha nodded, her eyes never leaving his. "I believe it. I've seen the way Caden reacts to the horses here. It's like he's connecting with them in a way he doesn't with most people."

"Horses are easier than people sometimes."

Her inquisitive gaze turned a bit playful. "Speaking from experience, I take it?"

Isaac felt a scowl forming before he could do anything about it. Tabitha wasn't prying, wasn't pushing him for more than he was willing to give, but the innocent question stirred up a tempest of raw emotions he wasn't prepared to deal with —least of all in front of her.

"I'm not much of a people person." Was that his voice that sounded so cold and unfriendly?

Her expression dimmed, and she averted her gaze, staring out at the paddock again. An awkward silence spread between them, feeling heavy and damp. Tabitha didn't need him to tell her he wasn't great at being a human anymore. She was getting a front-row seat right now.

When he couldn't take the silence anymore, he cleared his throat. "You seem to have figured life out pretty well. I'm sure it can't be easy raising a kid on your own."

Tabitha sighed, still avoiding his gaze. "It has its moments, but I've learned to adapt. And Caden… he teaches me more than I could ever teach him. He's got this way of seeing the world that's so unique and special, and I've come to appreciate that."

Isaac nodded, admiring her honesty as much as her resilience. "That's a good way to look at it," he said, meaning it.

Tabitha shrugged lightly. "I guess I've just learned that you have to find the good, wherever you can. Especially when things don't turn out the way you planned."

Isaac grunted, deep in reflection now. "Plans don't always work out the way we want."

"No, they don't," she said simply. "But sometimes the unexpected can be… better than what we thought we wanted."

He didn't say anything, mostly because of the sharp obstruction that seemed to be lodged in his throat. The only thing that came out of the unexpected for him had been heartbreak and loss. Such aching loss.

It clawed at him even now.

He wanted to make his excuses and step away from Tabitha before he either said something more to dampen her good spirits or, worse, made an even bigger fool of himself in front of her by wallowing in his grief and self-pity.

But as much as he felt the urge to hightail it back to his office for the rest of the day, his boots stayed put at the fence railing, and his gaze stayed fixed on Tabitha's little boy, who was completely mesmerized by the horses being shown to the kids in the paddock.

CHAPTER 7

The man was a little odd; there was no doubt about it.

He had ambled right over to her, so Tabitha figured she would be friendly, even after his abrupt parting the day before and silence at supper.

But now, after she had gone out of her way to say hello and stand by him, Isaac was staring off into space with an awful, strained expression. His eyes were all scrunched up, as if the sun was irritating them.

Tabitha bit down on her lower lip and turned back to where Caden was looking up at the horse, the counselor Ben right by his side. Caden was having the time of his life, and already he was excited to ride the horses, even though it would be a few days before the kids started actually riding.

All the articles were right: children on the spectrum were at ease around animals in a way they often weren't around other people.

Tabitha would focus on how well Caden was doing rather than stress over the stony silence of the man next to her.

She never was great at small talk and social interactions. Tabitha had been what some of the meaner kids in high school used to call a nerd. She was happiest either enjoying the quiet beauty of her family's ranch or holed up at her school library, learning how to code with the robotics team.

Even when she met David, he had done most of the flirting and pursuing. Tabitha had been easily swept away by his charm.

She internally shook her head. It felt weird to think about her ex-husband when Isaac was standing nearby.

Tabitha glanced at him, but he was still staring into the distance with that remote, unreachable look on his face.

She didn't know what she should say. She didn't want to force him to chat with her, and she certainly wasn't going to tell him that Caden had asked about him that morning.

Well, Caden hadn't used his name. He had asked Tabitha where the cowboy was. She had pointed over at Mateo, who was overseeing breakfast in the kitchen, but Caden had shaken his head.

"The other cowboy," he said. "Woody."

Tabitha smiled to herself, just thinking about it. She could only imagine what Isaac would think if he knew how her son was obsessed with him. Maybe Caden's mom was getting a little unhealthily interested in him too.

She was startled from her thoughts by Isaac finally clearing his throat.

"You seemed good with the horse," he said, still gazing out at the paddock. "Your ranch upbringing came back to you, I guess."

"It never really left." She laughed and relaxed somewhat as she thought about her childhood on the ranch back home.

"My mom always said riding horses was like riding a bicycle—it comes back to you, even after years away."

"I believe it." Isaac swiveled his head to look at her now, smiling softly. "I've never tested that theory, personally. I've never left the ranch for any length of time."

"I don't blame you. This place is great." Tabitha sighed. "My own family's ranch struggled a lot, truth be told. My parents had to sell about ten years ago and move somewhere smaller with just a few horses."

"Sorry to hear that. It happens often," Isaac said. "They just don't have enough money or people to keep big ranches going sometimes."

"Yes, and none of my sisters were up for the challenge." Tabitha leaned her forearms against the fence. "Not even me, to be honest. I wanted to see what else was out there."

She regretted her decision to leave home sometimes. She often wished she had stayed where it was safe and familiar, within the boundaries of her family home.

She was proud of everything she had accomplished, Caden included, but Tabitha sometimes thought she might have been spared a lot of pain and heartbreak if she had stayed home and made her life there instead. Then again, staying would have brought its own kind of sadness. Her sister Lisa stayed behind and had to help their parents sell the horses.

Tabitha had cried when Lisa described it. Some of those horses had been like members of the family.

"That sounds like my younger brother Sawyer." Isaac moved closer to her, just by an inch. "From the time he could walk, that one was dying to get out and travel the world."

"Sawyer? I didn't realize there was another Hart brother," Tabitha said. "That makes, what? Six boys?"

"Yup." Isaac chuckled. "And no girls."

"Your poor mother," Tabitha said. "I have my hands full with one boy. I can't imagine six."

Isaac furrowed his brow and seemed about to say something, but then just shrugged. Tabitha hoped he hadn't been about to point out what so many people had said, explicitly or implicitly, to her before—that Caden wasn't really the same as a "normal" child. Every child was unique, and every child presented their own set of challenges and wonders. Yes, Caden might have more needs, but he wasn't a burden or a hardship. And she hadn't meant to make it sound like he was too much for her.

"You seem to be a great mom." Isaac didn't quite look at her as he spoke it, but the comment still seemed genuine.

"Well, I hope you and your brothers manage to give your mother some granddaughters." Tabitha grinned, desperate to turn the conversation to a lighter topic. "For Vera's sake."

Instead of making him smile, Isaac's shoulders went tense as he turned his head away in a sudden movement.

The air between them seemed to turn cold, and Tabitha realized she had definitely said something wrong, but she couldn't for the life of her think what had changed his mood so sharply.

Was the subject of granddaughters somehow a thorny one? Or was it grandchildren in general? Maybe some of his brothers already had children from a previous relationship.

Tabitha's stomach turned queasy as she realized there could be a nasty divorce or breakup, possibly even a custody battle, and she had inadvertently brought up a sore personal topic for the family.

Or maybe it was something worse. Isaac himself could be involved in some sort of tense situation. Maybe he did have a child, and he or she was with the mother. Tabitha could have kicked herself.

This was why she hated small talk. She always put her foot in her mouth. In the silence that stretched out between them again, she wished the dusty earth would open up beneath her boots and swallow her.

"If I said something I shouldn't have, Isaac, I'm—"

"No grandkids yet." His voice was short and husky, as if it took great effort for him to speak. "But maybe one day. My brothers give Mom a lot of hope."

But not Isaac? Tabitha didn't ask the question that sat on the tip of her tongue. Instead, she nodded and looked back toward Caden, who was now reaching up to touch the horse's nose, his eyes aglow with delight.

At least she had confirmed one thing about Isaac. There was no custody battle between him and an ex. No mention of anyone in his life at all. That just made Isaac's reaction to her innocent question even stranger.

"So, you never took Caden riding out in California?" Isaac nodded toward the pasture.

Tabitha shook her head, grateful for the change in subject. "No, there aren't a lot of options, plus I've been focused on other forms of therapy with him so far."

"And you work full-time on top of all that? In web design, right?"

"Yes." Tabitha was surprised he knew that, but she supposed he had helped his mother organize the horsemanship program and probably knew the basics about all of the ranch's guests. "I can do my job remotely, so I'm really lucky," she said. "I just have to find time each day to hit my deadlines."

"When do you sleep?" Isaac tilted his head and quirked his mouth into a sideways smile.

He was so handsome that Tabitha couldn't help grinning up at him. When he was looking at her like that, all of his attention focused on her, she felt as if she were the only woman in the world. She didn't feel like an overtired mom but rather like a woman worth winning the attention of someone like Isaac Hart.

"It's true, I don't sleep," Tabitha quipped. "Please don't tell anyone. It's actually my superpower."

"Your secret's safe with me."

"Whew, thanks. Can't have that getting out." Tabitha swiped the back of her hand against her forehead as though in mock relief. Isaac chuckled, and she found herself staring into his warm gaze for a bit too long.

"What about Caden's dad?" Isaac's question was sudden. "Where's he while you two are here?"

Talk about feeling like someone had dunked her in freezing cold water. As much as she was enjoying talking with him, this was the one topic she didn't want to discuss with Isaac.

She sucked in her breath and turned away.

Isaac seemed like a kind and considerate man. She was sure he hadn't meant to pry. He probably just didn't know the details of how she became a single mother, and it was only natural to be curious.

She knew it was silly of her to get so upset by the question, but even so, it felt like Isaac had found the weak spot in her armor.

CHAPTER 8

The question had been too personal. Isaac knew that. In a twisted way, he felt a small burst of satisfaction at the clear discomfort in Tabitha's eyes. The conversation had been too good, too easy. He had found her too intriguing, too lovely. He had felt himself growing captivated by her presence. Even when she mentioned the prospect of granddaughters, he hadn't been upset.

He felt an inexplicable comfort around Tabitha. He felt he could share himself with her, and he craved to know her own secrets and feelings. He had even almost told her his whole pathetic story, but he refrained. She probably already thought he was strange enough without him unburdening on her after only knowing her a day.

So, he self-sabotaged. He couldn't keep drifting after her, so he figured it was best to nip it in the bud.

Instead, he had asked the question he had been dying to know from the moment he first saw Tabitha and her son. Because what kind of foolish man would leave an amazing woman like her, not to mention a great kid like Caden? What kind of man would abandon his child like that? No man at all, by Isaac's estimation. Whoever Caden's father was, he didn't deserve either one of them.

Still, Isaac felt bad for asking as soon as Tabitha sucked in a sharp breath. He had hurt her; he could tell. And shocked her with his bad manners.

She was proud, though. That was obvious as she lifted her chin and stared him down.

"I prefer not to talk about Caden's father, if you don't mind." Tabitha's voice was polite but firm.

Isaac nodded once. He understood. The conversation was over.

It had definitely been a bad move. Isaac reminded himself that it wasn't just about him. His mother wanted this program to be a success, and his unprofessional behavior with a guest was definitely not going to help in that endeavor.

Isaac took a deep breath and nodded. It was time for him to leave. He needed to lock himself back in his office and maybe not come out for six weeks. Any interaction with Tabitha was going to lead to him feeling awful and possibly the entire program failing.

He reached up and tipped his hat. Tabitha blinked, and she no longer seemed upset or uncomfortable, simply confused.

"I'm sorry," Isaac said. "I hope you have a good day."

Then he turned and walked as fast as he could back toward his office.

He hoped Tabitha didn't complain to his mother. First of all, Vera would come down on him with a fury over his asking personal questions about ex-husbands to a member of her cherished program.

And then Vera would ask questions of her own. She would want to know why Isaac, who was always so reserved and aloof, would ask such a personal question. She would dig, as no one but his mother could dig.

It would be unbearable. Isaac hoped Tabitha would just accept his apology and forget about him.

He would make it easy for her. For the next six weeks, he wouldn't so much as glance her way. He would never hang around the program or its participants. He would ensure he avoided it like the plague.

It would be easy. He already spent so many hours in the office anyway.

For all intents and purposes, Isaac would just disappear.

To his chagrin, Jacob, Mateo, and his dad were in the office when he returned. Jacob sat in one of the worn leather chairs, and Mateo was leaning against the desk next to Tom Hart.

Technically, the office didn't belong to only Isaac. It was shared between him and the rest of the family. And it had been his father's office since the founding of the ranch. As a rule, it was typically busier in the afternoon, with people coming in and out to pick up checks or file receipts of sale.

"Where were you just now?" Jacob raised his brows, clearly curious.

"Just taking a walk, checking things out at the paddocks." Isaac moved to another chair and sat down. "Came back here to get some more work done."

"I'm driving over to see a new foal at Gary's ranch," Jacob said. "Come join me, and we'll get supper at the diner."

Jacob had recently told Elizabeth that she didn't need to work at the diner anymore now that they were getting married, but she insisted on keeping her part-time job. She liked her independence, and she was currently a huge favorite among the locals, thanks to her sweet disposition.

Isaac hesitated. On the one hand, he didn't want to subject

himself to his brother's inevitable questions and prodding. On the other, if he hung around the office and the ranch, who knew if he would be able to resist seeking out Tabitha?

That made his decision easy.

"All right, I'll come," Isaac said.

"Excellent." Jacob sprang to his feet. "Mateo, you in?"

"I'm picking up Claire later."

"Right, right, of course." Jacob gave Mateo a teasing smile, but they all knew it was in good fun. There was nothing Mateo would rather do than drive his fiancée Claire around.

At first, the whole family had worried about how Mateo seemed to wait on Claire hand and foot, and Isaac himself had uttered some words he deeply regretted. He had let his own pain cloud his judgment. He had assumed that Claire would hurt Mateo because, in his experience, love and devotion like the kind Mateo had for Claire only led to heartbreak.

It turned out, Claire gave Mateo happiness and comfort beyond what they could have imagined, and none of them had ever seen their cousin and adopted brother so content.

"Here." Their father lifted up a piece of paper filled with his familiar scrawl. "A list of things to pick up at the supply store."

Fifteen minutes later, Jacob and Isaac were in Jacob's truck, bound for a neighboring ranch.

"So it looks like Mom's program is going well so far." Jacob steered his truck with one hand and kept throwing looks at Isaac.

"Yup." Isaac nodded and tried to fixate on the familiar surrounding land.

There had been a time when Isaac talked to his older brother about everything. They were close in age, and living at the ranch, they had been friends as well as brothers.

Jacob was the first person Isaac had told when he was going to propose to Anna. Jacob was shocked but happy. He'd told Isaac that he would never marry unless he found a love like Isaac and Anna shared.

And now Jacob had found just that, but he rarely talked about it with Isaac. Jacob was probably trying to be kind. Jacob was always thinking of others. He likely didn't want to rub his own happiness in Isaac's face.

It only made the distance between them feel that much bigger.

"They seem nice, all the parents and kids, especially Tabitha." Jacob was never subtle. "Mom said she thinks she's around thirty-one. So, just a few years younger than you."

"Don't." Isaac meant to speak quietly and in a monotone voice, to show Jacob how little he cared, but the word came out sharp and harsh. There was no pretending he wasn't emotional at the mention of Tabitha.

Jacob took a breath so deep that his chest rose and fell. "Isaac, I know you. You've changed, it's true, but you're still my brother, and I still know you as well as I know my own hand."

Isaac kept his head bent down. This was typical. Every few months, Jacob would try to break through the barriers between them. Jacob wanted Isaac to be more like his old self. He wanted Isaac to laugh and joke and join his brothers on wild romps like he used to. It was useless. The person Isaac had been back then had died with Anna and the baby, Alice.

"I know you like Tabitha." Jacob spoke with certainty.

Isaac jerked his head up, unable to mask his surprise. Jacob had only been at the supper with the guests that first night. Isaac hadn't uttered a word to Tabitha the whole evening.

Jacob gave him a wry grin and shrugged. "You sneaked

looks at her all through supper as if you would die if anyone caught you looking. Plus, Mom mentioned you carried her luggage all the way to the guesthouse."

"I carried everyone's luggage to the guesthouse," Isaac pointed out. "I'm helping Mom out with the program."

"Did you hang back to chat with all the other guests?"

Isaac couldn't help but scoff and roll his eyes, but he was smiling.

"My point is, you like her, and that's not a bad thing." Jacob lowered his voice. "You shouldn't try to dampen your natural feelings."

"Stop." Isaac shook his head. "Please stop."

Jacob opened his mouth to say more, but something in Isaac's pained expression made him pause.

Isaac replayed the scene between him and Tabitha earlier. How it had been going well for a few minutes until he went too far. Until he dug into her painful past.

If Jacob had witnessed that, he wouldn't be pushing Isaac toward her with such enthusiasm. It was obvious Isaac was unfit for dating anyone. He had lost the ability to even carry on a polite conversation.

"I never ask you for anything," Isaac muttered. "But I'm asking you now. Don't push me on this."

Jacob swallowed hard. Isaac spoke the truth. For years, his family had offered him everything. The sun and the moon. All out of pity. Isaac never took any of their offers, nor did he ask. He simply gave what he had to the ranch. And Jacob knew that.

So Jacob turned his attention back to the road, and he didn't speak about Tabitha for the rest of the trip.

CHAPTER 9

Tabitha couldn't have imagined a better two weeks. Days spent at Hart's Ridge Ranch seemed to fly by. Every morning, she and Caden woke up excited about what the day had in store, and every evening, they collapsed into bed, exhausted from hours spent outdoors with the horses.

The time they didn't spend with the horses was just as well-planned. Donna and the counselors took the kids for nature hikes, and they had daily sessions on communication skills, similar to the classes Caden attended back in California.

The counselors tutored the kids as well, usually after working with the horses, and Tabitha noticed Caden seemed much better at focusing on his schoolwork than usual. Already, his reading skills were improving, and his math abilities, which had been impressive to begin with, were exceeding Tabitha's wildest expectations.

Tabitha trusted the counselors and their capabilities so much that she felt comfortable leaving Caden with them for a few hours each day so she could take care of her own work.

In the evening, after putting Caden to bed, she stayed up to jot down notes on the program and everything she liked about it. She definitely wanted to blog about it and maybe post on a community forum at the very least. She had become a true fan of Hart's Ridge Ranch, and she wanted to spread the word about the excellent program Vera was running, especially since Vera had told her she had ambitions to expand and offer the program year-round.

Tabitha had learned the Harts never did anything halfway at the ranch. Tom Hart was renowned for being one of the best horse handlers in the area. He had an expert eye when it came to breeding, buying, and selling, and it was said that he could train horses that others had deemed totally unmanageable.

Over many shared meals, Tabitha had learned all about the development of the ranch, and how Tom and Vera had grown it from a small bit of land into the massive operation it was today. Every son played a role, too, except for the one who was off traveling the world.

She learned more about Isaac as well, though only surface-level things. All in all, the man remained a total mystery to her. She had seen him from a distance, entering or exiting the stables, or grabbing his food quickly at supper, but he hadn't talked to her since that second day and their conversation that had been so nice until it turned awkward.

Vera explained that Isaac handled all of the administrative-type tasks for the ranch: budgeting, payroll, taxes.

All the boring stuff, it sounded like.

He had done a lot to organize the children's horsemanship program, but it was all behind-the-scenes work that seemed to keep him isolated in his work.

So Tabitha supposed it wasn't odd that she had barely glimpsed him after their exchange by the paddock.

Except she couldn't help thinking he was avoiding her.

Most of the suppers were shared meals with the entire Hart family. Isaac was either absent at those suppers lately, or he came and went so fast he barely exchanged words with anyone, much less Tabitha.

His family, however, seemed totally used to his elusiveness. In fact, it was as if Isaac was the resident ghost. He was there, but something about his presence seemed insubstantial. As if he was a shadow of an actual person.

Tabitha told herself to put Isaac out of her mind as the third week of the program started. She instead listened to Caden explain over breakfast how leather was made, something he'd learned in yesterday's lessons. Like many children on the spectrum, he tended to fixate on certain topics. Lately, he had been obsessed with how everyday objects were made. Tabitha loved to see him so enthused and engaged, so she was always eager to listen and help him with his research. She watched with pride at how quickly he memorized facts.

Across the guesthouse table from them, Daisy nodded along to Caden's monologuing and delicately ate her scrambled eggs and ketchup.

Cindy sipped her coffee and passed some overnight oats to Tabitha. All the parents were taking turns fixing breakfast on the days they ate at the guesthouse.

"Ben says they might go on a trail ride this week," Cindy said.

A few weeks ago, the thought of Caden on a horse in the woods might have terrified Tabitha, but the counselors took every precaution when it came to the kids' safety and well-being. Not only were the program's horses extremely placid and gentle animals, but whenever a child was riding, their horse was led by a counselor on either side for safety.

"Ben!" Caden stopped talking about leather mid-sentence to shout the name of his favorite counselor. "Where's Ben?"

"He'll be in the paddock later, sweetheart." Tabitha wanted to pat Caden's back to comfort him, but he didn't like being touched without warning. They only hugged at specific times and when he formally requested it. It was strange to Tabitha at first to not be able to touch her child when it felt natural to her, but she had adjusted to it. Each touch and hug was all the more precious for how long she sometimes had to wait for it. "Finish your breakfast, and we'll get to see Ben and the others, okay?"

Caden happily dug into his pancakes with exactly two tablespoons of maple syrup, his preferred breakfast.

Ben was becoming his favorite now that Isaac rarely came around. Over the course of the last couple of weeks, Tabitha had also gotten to know the counselor who was about her age. Ben had grown up with an autistic sibling, and after college, he became passionate about physical therapy programs. He had spent the last decade hopping from program to program, many of which involved horses. He was very good at interacting with the children, which was no surprise, given his personal experience.

He definitely liked Caden as well. Cindy had even teased that Ben had a bit of a crush on Tabitha, but Tabitha had brushed that off. Ben was just a friendly guy.

And he wasn't her type.

Tabitha was terrified to think it, never mind say it out loud, but Isaac Hart was actually more her type. If she even had a type. It had been so long since she'd even considered dating or relationships, she wasn't sure of anything anymore.

Which probably explained why she couldn't stop thinking about a grim, mysterious loner like Isaac Hart.

The kicker was, she had gotten the feeling that he might have been a little bit interested in her too. Until their awkward conversation when she had clammed up at the mention of her ex. She'd probably given him the idea that she was still hung up on Caden's father, based on her chilly reaction. Maybe that was partly why Isaac was steering clear of her now.

Tabitha had the strangest urge to explain herself to him. To tell Isaac about her divorce and how Caden was better without any father than one who would view him as a burden.

After all, she and Isaac were having a pretty nice time together before the specter of her ex entered the conversation. Isaac had just been trying to get to know her. Looking back on it now, Tabitha realized there had been no judgment. He had just been curious about her and wanted to know more. She was the one who had overreacted.

Tabitha knew better than anyone that not everyone had the same set of social skills—herself included. So, she should have had a little more patience for Isaac asking a question that was uncomfortable for her. She also was starting to think that if she hadn't been so awkward after he asked, he might have spoken to her again. And she very much wanted that.

Tabitha had been divorced for years. Why couldn't she just have flashed a breezy smile and said that? Instead, she had gone silent as if there were some lingering feelings for her ex.

She knew what she was feeling for Isaac was just a foolish crush that could never go anywhere, but Tabitha craved his company. There had been something so delightful about a few exchanged smiles with the soft-spoken, kind, and handsome man.

As Tabitha and Caden headed with Cindy and Daisy to the first session of the day, Tabitha mulled over how she might apologize to Isaac. She had no desire to wander around the ranch looking for him, even though Vera and Tom had made it clear that the parents were welcome to take walks in their free time, as long as they avoided certain horses being kept in specific and clearly marked areas for the untrained and tempestuous animals.

A few times, Tabitha had witnessed Diane, Beau's girlfriend and a gifted trainer, working with one such stallion. Beautiful, blonde Diane was capable and cautious, but even from a safe distance Tabitha had still shivered with a mix of fear and excitement as the young woman stroked the temperamental animal's nose. The stallion had such raw power, and so much emotion seemed to live behind his eyes.

Standing on the porch of the guesthouse, Tabitha watched Caden run off to greet Ben, probably to tell him new facts about leather making. The boy would bend the counselor's ear for an hour, given the chance. Ben looked over and waved at Tabitha, signaling that Caden was safe in his care for a while.

Which left Tabitha on her own for a bit. Her thoughts turned swiftly to Isaac. Should she wander over to the barn where his office was and try to break the ice? Even if she found him, what would she say? He would probably think it was weird that she sought him out to apologize.

It would all be much simpler if he was more present around the program. She saw at least two of his brothers at the ranch every day. She had exchanged pleasantries with all of them, and she even had several longer conversations with Jacob and his fiancée, Elizabeth.

If Isaac deigned to actually spend an entire meal with

everyone else, it might be easy for Tabitha to casually mention she was sorry about how awkward she had been. And if he wanted to maybe talk with her another time, that might be nice too. Maybe they could be friends.

Tabitha sighed and shook her head. She was being silly. What she wanted from Isaac was definitely more than friendship.

For the first time in an awfully long time, she was attracted to a man. It shocked her to realize it, but there it was. Tabitha thought she was too old to yearn for romance. Maybe not literally too old, but definitely too tired. Too focused on Caden and the responsibility of providing a good life for him, especially now that it was just the two of them. He had been her sole focus for so long, it felt strange to remember she was also a woman with her own needs and desires. She had also thought she would never meet someone who made her want to flirt and slow dance and share candlelit meals. Unfortunately for her, that man happened to be the elusive Isaac Hart.

Tabitha settled in on the porch and watched as Caden joined the other kids on the broad lawn for the first session of the day. He was so engrossed in the activities he barely spared her a glance.

Something tugged at her heartstrings to see him so independent. For so long, she had needed to be by his side.

If she'd ever had a doubt if the program at Hart's Ridge Ranch would be helpful to him, there was no debating it now. Caden was flourishing here. Enrolling him in the program had been one of the best decisions she'd ever made for her son.

But in a few more weeks, she and Caden would go back to California. Back to their real life, which was hundreds of miles away from this idyllic corner of Wyoming. She would find a way to continue Caden's horse therapy back home. Maybe she would even return to Hart's Ridge Ranch for another program at some point.

Watching him now was just the reality check she needed.

Caden was everything to her. Rather than daydreaming about Isaac Hart, she should be savoring every moment of her son's enjoyment while they were at Hart's Ridge Ranch.

And so she would.

CHAPTER 10

Isaac had been pulled from his office against his will by his mother. She needed help setting up for an afternoon picnic for the program, and apparently, she couldn't find any other sons to help move benches and tables.

Isaac felt he had been doing an excellent job of avoiding Tabitha Young for several days, so he was miffed at his mother for dragging him to the wide back lawn.

Even so, it was a sunny and mild day, as if the universe knew Vera had planned for such a picnic, and Isaac couldn't help but enjoy being outdoors. He had been cooped up in his office for twice his usual amount of time in his desperation to not run into Tabitha again.

The one blessing was that Jacob hadn't brought her up again after their conversation. Isaac was shocked his brother had suggested he start dating again, in the first place. Clearly, Isaac's plea to drop the subject and never bring it up again had chastised Jacob. He was back to letting Isaac hole up in the office for hours on end and skip family meals.

Isaac knew, though, that if his older brother caught him

chatting with Tabitha, or even looking in her direction, Jacob would return to the topic.

Isaac couldn't let that happen. He went to every length to avoid Tabitha's presence. That didn't mean she wasn't in his thoughts.

Isaac thought about her constantly. He never asked about her, but when his mother mentioned Tabitha or Caden while discussing the program, Isaac's ears perked up. He was happy when he heard that Caden was loving the horseback riding. When he found out that Tabitha sometimes posted on online forums and blogs about her experiences raising an autistic child, Isaac had broken one of his own personal rules and looked her up.

His heart had been racing with the fear that someone would walk into the office while he was typing her name into the computer. Even though he did the search early in the morning when he knew the stables were basically empty, and the screen was facing away from the door, he was still in a panic.

He couldn't stop himself from searching for her and then reading every single thing she had posted online.

It was a mistake. After he read her thoughtful review of a program Caden did in California, he had to know more. So, then he read her guest post on another mother's popular blog, and another one. He even read her bio on her job's website, discovering she had amazing graphic art and web design skills. He lost track of the time as he continued his snooping and came away from the experience feeling both guilty and deeply impressed by her.

Maybe even more troubling, he realized he liked her. It wasn't just lust and physical attraction, although it was impossible to deny that she was an incredibly beautiful, desirable woman. He admired and respected Tabitha Young as a person.

And that was far more dangerous than just being attracted to her.

Tabitha was smart and kind and accomplished. She wrote with thoughtfulness and just the right amount of humor. Her technical skills were uniquely her as well.

Isaac had closed the tabs and wiped the search history on the computer, just as Vera stepped into the open doorway of his office.

"Whatever you're doing in here will have to wait. We've got to get those tables set up."

"I was just on my way," he said, hoping his five o'clock shadow helped hide some of the heat he felt in his face.

His mother walked ahead of him, pointing like a drill sergeant. "I want that pair of tables moved over there on the even ground. And spread some blankets out over here."

Isaac nodded and moved the tables where his mother directed. If he acted quickly, with any luck, he could be well out of the vicinity by the time the program guests showed up. Vera informed him they had just finished a riding session and had all gone back to the guesthouse to wash up.

"Mateo!" His mother called across the lawn. "Set up the grill here."

Isaac turned to see Mateo wheeling out the grill with help from his fiancée, Claire. Isaac smiled to himself at the sight of Claire in her pink button-down over cropped jeans and sandals. Not exactly ranch attire, but it didn't seem to slow her down. It wasn't so long ago that Isaac had disregarded former beauty queen Claire Hawkins as shallow and unserious, but now he recognized she was a strong-willed woman who wouldn't compromise who she was just to fit in with others. She also happened to adore Mateo, which was good enough for Isaac.

"Hi, guys." Claire's chipper voice rang out. "We've got hot dogs and burgers and tons of fresh produce back in the truck."

"Claire also bought out the whole aisle of chips," Mateo joked.

"Hey, I know how to plan a party," she quipped, then helped Mateo set down the grill. Isaac turned away as Mateo threw his arms around Claire and pulled her close for a kiss.

No one deserved to find their special person more than his cousin Mateo. Of all his brothers, Mateo was the one who could best understand Isaac's loss. Years ago, when he was a little boy, Mateo had lost his own biological mother. Mateo had gone through a phase of being quiet and withdrawn as a child, and he suffered from nightmares.

So Mateo had been the most patient when Isaac changed after losing Anna and the baby. He never pushed or pressed. He always gave Isaac the space he needed. It was as if Mateo understood that some wounds could not heal.

Isaac would never wish unhappiness on Mateo, but part of him had always believed that Mateo would never settle down. It was clear to everyone that Mateo was hung up on Claire since high school, but it also seemed obvious that she was never going to choose him, especially when she had married someone else.

The union hadn't lasted, and after Mateo learned Claire was single again, he hadn't let anything—or anyone—stand in the way of winning her heart.

Of course, Isaac was happy for Mateo and Claire, but it also made him feel lonely.

Vera stood with her hands on her hips as she ordered her sons around. "All right, Mateo, get the grill started. Isaac, you go get the rest of the food from Mateo's truck. Claire, help me with these blankets, would you, please? I need your eye for making things pretty and cozy."

Isaac sighed and headed for his brother's vehicle. There was no point in arguing that he had things to do in his office. His mother was determined to enlist all her sons and their significant others to make this picnic a success. It was a celebration of sorts to mark the first two weeks of the program. Isaac knew his mother deserved a good evening as much as their guests. The program was an enormous hit. Even he could tell that from the distance he'd been keeping.

When he returned with the food for the grill, the other counselors were already gathered. Luke, the oldest student in the program, was already there as well, watching Mateo explain how the grill worked.

As Mateo started cooking, the smoky smell of barbecue drifted through the air, and Isaac lingered. He figured he might as well stay for a burger. It would be odd if he left now. Plus, he was hungry after hours of working in his office.

Deep down, despite all his doubts and reservations, he had to admit he also wanted just a glimpse of Tabitha.

When she arrived, Isaac felt every muscle in his body shift. He was desperate to walk over to where she and Caden were taking some food off the serving table. Isaac had the inexplicable urge to walk over and offer to hold her plate for her. To ask how her day had been. To just be next to her for a moment.

She was wearing a simple, white short-sleeve blouse and pants made out of a loose and flowy fabric. Caden, meanwhile, was dressed as he had insisted on dressing every day: blue jeans, a blue button-down, his small cowboy boots, and a blue hat placed atop his head.

Tabitha leaned down to ask him something about his foot, and he nodded and pointed.

Isaac was smiling at the sight of them before he could stop himself.

The smile instantly faded as Ben, one of the counselors, approached the two of them. Caden looked up and started chattering with enthusiasm, and Ben and Tabitha shared a warm smile. Ben was standing close to her, as close as he could without touching.

The sight made Isaac want to punch his fist through a wall.

They had obviously become friends over the last few weeks. Possibly more than friends.

While Isaac fixated on every minute movement of Ben and Tabitha, his brother Liam ambled up beside him.

"Jealous, huh?" Liam raised his brows and elbowed Isaac playfully.

Isaac started and shook his head. "I don't know what you're talking about."

"In case you're wondering, I don't think there's anything romantic between them." Liam could always be counted on to know the gossip around the ranch. "At least not yet."

"Liam, drop it."

Liam cocked his head and studied Isaac. "It's okay to start living again, you know."

"What's that supposed to mean?" Isaac turned toward his brother, his tone harsh.

Liam was unbothered. He simply shrugged. "You smile every time you see Tabitha. You even smile when you're watching her kid. Clearly, you still have the ability to be happy."

Isaac narrowed his eyes in anger. Liam knew nothing about how Isaac felt or what he did or didn't have the ability for. Liam was an optimist; he always had been. He saw the glass as half full. He looked for a silver lining in everything. Isaac wouldn't have his brother any other way, but then again, life had been easy for Liam. Isaac hoped his younger brother never had a reason to lose his optimism. That didn't mean Isaac didn't find it highly annoying at the moment.

The worst part was that Liam was almost right. Isaac was drawn to Tabitha. Thinking about her, simply looking at her, made him happy.

He couldn't argue with what Liam was saying. And maybe, in another life, in another universe, Tabitha would be the type of woman Isaac would approach. Maybe she would be a woman he could fall in love with.

But he didn't have another life. He only had the ruins that were left of his life after losing his wife and unborn child. He had nothing good to offer Tabitha, and she deserved a man who could give her everything and more.

All of those feelings and regrets boiled up inside him as he looked at Liam.

"I'll thank you to leave me alone about this, brother. You don't have the experience to know what I'm feeling. I pray you never will know it."

Isaac left Liam standing there without another word and walked toward the table of food.

Even as Isaac put every effort into not looking toward Tabitha, it was as if all his other senses were heightened and attuned to her. He could hear her laughing somewhere behind him. He could sense her presence like an electric current that was impossible to ignore.

He piled his plate with food and then took a seat at the far edge of the picnic table, across from Mateo and Claire. Mateo gave him a look, a puzzled expression on his face, but kept his mouth shut. Claire studiously avoided eye contact. Both of them could tell Isaac was in a bad mood.

He looked up, over Claire's shoulder, and he saw Tabitha. Only this time, she was looking at him. She was sitting cross-legged on a blanket, Caden at her side, and Ben on the other side of the boy. Tabitha held a plate of food, but she wasn't eating. She was just looking at Isaac.

For one charged second, they held eye contact. She was a few yards away, but there was no doubt that she was looking at him. Her lips were parted slightly, as if she was about to say something.

In an instant, it was over. Tabitha looked away, her cheeks turning slightly red.

Ben said something that drew her attention away from Isaac, and she didn't look back again.

Isaac told himself it would be good if she and Ben spent more time together. Good for her, and good for Isaac too. Caden obviously liked the personable, good-looking counselor.

So, why did watching them together make Isaac's mouth go dry as dust? Why did his chest feel as though a heavy weight were settling on it?

Isaac was sure he didn't want to know.

CHAPTER 11

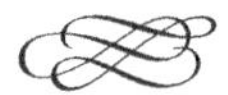

The more Tabitha told herself to just ignore Isaac, the more she was tempted to look at him.

He had been like a ghost for two weeks. She would have never expected him to show up at the picnic. Yet there he was, as handsome as ever, seated across from Mateo and Claire.

And he'd been looking at her. Still was, though he seemed to be pretending he wasn't. Tabitha couldn't say how she knew for certain that his eyes were on her, but she kept feeling a warm, tickling sensation at the back of her neck. Isaac's gaze was as palpable as a caress—even when he was glowering slightly.

Ben was saying something to her, but his words blurred out under her inattention. Tabitha could only think about Isaac.

She glanced at Ben and saw that he was waiting for her to respond to whatever he had said.

"Sorry, what was that?" Tabitha asked.

"I just said it might be fun to take Caden into town to see the stores and the diner. I think he'd like it."

"Oh, yes, that would be nice." Tabitha set her plate of barely touched food down on the blanket next to where she sat. "I think Vera mentioned a group field trip later this week."

"Yeah, but we could always take Caden on our own during your free time," Ben said.

Tabitha blinked over at the counselor. He had been friendly to her and Caden, but this offer was a surprise. Of course, it could just be the continuation of his general friendliness, but she also sensed he was asking for something more. A date?

She nearly choked on the idea. Cindy had teased her about Ben having a crush, but Tabitha had brushed those comments off. Now she wasn't so sure.

She didn't know what to say. Before she responded, she realized with a jolt that Caden had wandered away from their blanket. All thoughts of Ben vanished from her head as she scanned her surroundings for her child.

Tabitha swiveled her head around, and then she spotted him. He was making a beeline for the big picnic table. Right to where Isaac Hart was sitting.

She sucked in a breath, though more out of embarrassment than worry.

Caden wasn't in any danger here, so she relaxed marginally, but she was also desperate to call her son back before he bothered Isaac. She knew from experience, though, that shouting out at Caden rarely made him listen or obey.

So all she could do was hold her breath as she watched him pull to a stop right in front of Isaac and give him a long look.

Caden said something, and even straining her ears, Tabitha didn't quite hear it.

Part of her was terrified that Isaac would be cold and look

away, shutting her son out the way he had her. Tabitha was a grown adult, yet Isaac's stoniness had hurt her. She hated to think what it would do to Caden, who still adored the man. He looked up to Isaac because he loved cowboys, and Isaac was even more special because he was a real cowboy.

But Isaac didn't reject her son. His handsome face broke into a warm smile, transforming the gloom that had been on his face when Tabitha had caught him watching her earlier. He leaned down and answered Caden's question, pointing at his boots. Caden must have asked him about how they were made.

Tabitha felt a mix of emotions as she watched the sweet exchange. She was filled with joy over Isaac's kind reception toward Caden, yet a strange sadness grew inside her. Why did Isaac smile so easily at Caden while he ignored her?

She felt like a fool, being jealous of her six-year-old son, but she couldn't deny the feeling for what it was. Tabitha had felt the warmth of Isaac's smile on her before; she knew how wonderful it felt to be the focus of his attention. He had looked at her and made her feel seen. She had been craving that feeling again the past couple of weeks, but he hadn't returned to her. He must not have felt the connection she did.

And seeing Isaac give such kindness to her son was like dangling it right in front of her face, yet just out of reach. A beautiful gift, but not for her.

Tabitha watched as Isaac shifted to the side, and Caden climbed up on the bench beside him. Caden propped his chin on his hand and peppered Isaac with questions. From where she sat, Tabitha heard some of the phrases. Caden wanted to know how many horses Isaac had ever ridden. Isaac tilted his head, giving it serious thought, before he answered. Tabitha could tell by the way Caden furrowed his little brow that Isaac hadn't given an exact answer. After all, Isaac had probably been riding since he was a child—there was no way he could know for certain.

Caden kept pushing back. Her son liked certainties. Hard facts and data. Definite numbers. Feelings and estimates were more difficult for him.

Isaac didn't lose patience, though. He continued to chat with Caden as if it were the most important conversation in his world.

A lump grew in Tabitha's throat. She knew she should stop staring like an obsessive helicopter parent. Caden had interacted with plenty of the people at the ranch in the past few weeks, and she hadn't fixated on any of those conversations. She couldn't look away, though.

She noticed the subtle expressions of surprise on the faces of Mateo and Claire, who were sitting near Isaac. So, his interaction with Caden was shocking to them as well? Tabitha tucked that piece of information away with all the other small ways in which Isaac seemed to be regarded as a ghost by his family.

In her wildest and most secret dreams, Tabitha had hoped she might meet someone new. A man who would love her and love Caden too. A man who would help her when she was overwhelmed. A man who would be a real father to Caden, not just a person who sent child support checks and demonstrated his fatherhood with occasional presents or quick visits.

Tabitha hadn't truly believed she could meet such a man. She still didn't. Yet as she watched Isaac talk to her son, that impossible dream seemed more tangible than ever.

She had been so fixated on her son and Isaac she didn't

even realize that Ben had gotten up from the blanket at some point and strayed off to another area of the picnic.

All the other family members, guests, and children were absorbed in their own worlds. Luke and his parents were playing a game of cornhole. Cindy was chatting with some of the counselors while Daisy ate. Other program parents talked amongst themselves or helped their kids through the meal.

Tabitha's gaze drifted to Vera. Of all the people gathered, Vera Hart was the only one who kept turning her head to look at Isaac and Caden. She seemed almost as transfixed as Tabitha to see her adult son and the little boy talking so easily together. In fact, the woman looked nearly as emotional as Tabitha felt. Vera was managing to nod along to a conversation with Donna and a few other counselors, but her eyes seemed a bit glassy as she continuously flicked her attention toward Isaac.

Tabitha wondered why the sight of Isaac with a child would cause such a strong reaction in his mother.

She recalled how stiff Isaac had gotten when Tabitha joked about grandchildren. There was definitely something going on there. Tabitha couldn't guess what, though, and she certainly didn't want to ask outright. That wasn't her place.

The sun was low in the sky, and the twilight air was heavy and cool and pleasant. Tabitha looked out at the pink-and-purple horizon, at the horses grazing in the huge pastures, and she thought she had never seen anything so beautiful.

Then she turned back to Caden, seeing his eyes filled with excitement as he continued to chatter at Isaac, and Tabitha felt her heart begin to melt.

She knew better than to hope. She was only setting herself up for heartbreak. Ever since Caden was born, Tabitha had told herself that he was the priority. Caden was more than enough. She didn't need a man in her life too. She didn't need to invite any drama or confusing relationship dynamics into their life. Caden needed stability. He didn't need a distracted mother.

Tabitha pushed herself onto her knees. She needed to take a walk. Caden was in good hands for the time being, and Tabitha could ask Cindy to keep an eye on him for a few minutes.

She just couldn't sit here and watch him with Isaac and let herself get carried away with the thought of a future that was highly unlikely. The man had only spoken to her a handful of times, and lately he had barely looked at her, yet here she was tempted to imagine an entire life with him.

It was dangerous and pointless.

Tabitha was about to push herself to her feet when Caden called for her.

"Mommy!" His voice carried across the lawn. "Mommy, come here!"

Tabitha felt as if she moved in slow motion as she looked over.

Caden was still seated by Isaac's side, but Mateo and Claire had left, leaving Isaac and Caden alone at the picnic table. Caden was waving her over, his face lit up with excitement. She knew that face. He had learned a new fact that he was excited to share with her.

Tabitha could never say no to that face. She could never ignore her son's call.

Her stomach flipped as she looked at Isaac's unreadable face. He probably didn't want to talk to her. She would feel like she was imposing. He hadn't even meant to talk to Caden, but her son had practically ambushed him.

And now he was going to be stuck with both of them.

Tabitha told herself she would extricate herself and Caden as soon as possible. Caden was obsessed with Isaac, but Tabitha would try and convince him to walk down to look at the horses or something. She wouldn't annoy Isaac any longer than necessary, even if pulling Caden away caused a meltdown.

Then she looked at Isaac's face again. Really looked. He didn't seem annoyed or angry. He didn't look like he didn't want to spend time with her.

Instead, he looked hopeful. As if he, too, wanted Tabitha to join them. There was a lightness to his expression that Tabitha had never seen, and he was still smiling over whatever Caden had been saying to him.

Tabitha doubted anyone else was paying attention, but to her, it felt like she was in some sort of slow-motion scene from a movie. Every step toward Isaac and Caden felt nothing less than monumental.

CHAPTER 12

Isaac hadn't meant to talk with Caden for so long. But the boy had been so eager and endearing as he pulled himself up on the bench, then proceeded to ask endless questions about all the horses Isaac had ridden in his life.

Before Isaac knew it, Mateo and Claire had drifted away, and it was just Caden and him. And, honestly, he hadn't minded. Talking to the boy was the most stress-free conversation Isaac had enjoyed in a very long time.

When Caden abruptly called Tabitha over, Isaac's heart had just about leapt out of his chest. Not with dread, even though spending time with Tabitha was the very thing he wanted to avoid. The galloping of his heartbeat had been due to excitement.

She drifted over with her graceful yet steady stride, her eyes wide and curious, her dark hair blowing gently in the soft breeze. She sat across from them at the picnic table, sending a shy glance in Isaac's direction. Her pretty mouth quirked, as if she wanted to smile at him but was unsure how he might react to her.

Little wonder, Isaac acknowledged, as he recalled the strained ending to their previous conversation weeks prior.

"Afternoon, Tabitha." He smiled at her, trying to reassure her that he wasn't going to ask more prying questions or make her feel uncomfortable.

"Hi, Isaac." The smile she gave him in return was radiant. She pushed her long hair over her shoulder as she leaned on her elbows and looked at Caden. "What have you two been talking about over here?"

"Horses!" Caden exclaimed, his eyes lit up as he beamed at his mother. "Guess how many Isaac's rode, Mom."

Tabitha pretended to give the question serious thought. "Oh, I imagine that's a big number, right?"

"How many?" Caden pressed.

"Hm… Is it more than twenty?"

Caden splayed his hands, indicating the number was much bigger. "More than a hundred!"

Tabitha responded with wide-eyed disbelief. "Well, that's a lot of horses, isn't it?"

She glanced at Isaac again, an expression of warmth and gratitude in her lovely face. He cast around for something to add to the conversation, wanting to be part of it and not just an observer.

"I told Caden I couldn't be precisely sure of the number, since I never really stopped to count them all up."

"I wouldn't lose count." Caden shook his head. "I've rode two horses since we got here. There's Bluebell, for one. I rode him twelve times. And Lilac for five times. That's two horses and seventeen rides."

Isaac smiled at him. "I think you're better at counting than I was at your age."

Caden turned his head quickly toward Isaac. "How old are you?"

"Caden… Isaac might not want to say." Tabitha's cheeks turned a pretty shade of pink that almost exactly matched the sunset behind her.

"I'm thirty-four." Isaac shrugged. "I don't mind saying."

"That's three years older than my mommy." Caden grinned over at Tabitha. He was clearly proud of his math skills and unbothered by his mother's spreading blush.

"That's exactly right, sweetheart," Tabitha said.

She folded her hands together, and her eyes darted to Isaac and away again as she looked back to Caden. "Do you want a cookie for dessert? We can go grab some at the table over there."

Caden hopped off the bench. "I can get it myself."

Isaac chuckled at the boy's pride and determination to be independent. "Hey, Caden, would you get one for me too? And maybe one for your mom?"

"Sure!" Caden nodded once and then darted away, racing toward the table that was filled with homemade cookies and brownies. Elizabeth and Vera had been baking all afternoon.

"If he's bothering you with all his questions," Tabitha said, "I can take him back to the guesthouse. It's nearly time for him to wind down for the night, anyway."

Isaac instantly understood why she had suggested a cookie. She thought Caden was a nuisance to Isaac. The fact was completely the opposite. Isaac wanted Tabitha to know that. The rational part of him knew it would be wiser to let her walk away, but he couldn't live with himself if he made her think Caden was in any way bothersome. In fact, the time he had just spent with Caden had been one of the best parts of his month. Second only to the short time Isaac had spent with Tabitha.

He shook his head. "I'm having a nice time with him."

"Really?" Tabitha looked so hopeful and happy.

"Yes. He's no bother at all, I promise." Isaac cleared his throat, uncomfortable with the clear joy emanating from Tabitha at his simple statement. "So, how has the program been so far?"

"Oh, it's been great." Some of the tension drained out of Tabitha as she leaned forward. "Caden loves it, and everything has been really well-organized."

"And you've had time to work, too, right? You work remotely?"

"Yes." Her brows rose, as if she were surprised he knew about her job. "More time than I even expected. I know I can leave Caden with the counselors. They're all so capable and kind."

Isaac wondered if she was thinking specifically of Ben when she praised the counselors. He had seen the way Ben looked at her, like a lovesick puppy. Probably not too far off from the way Isaac was looking at her now.

Although Isaac noted with some satisfaction, Tabitha had seemed largely indifferent and unaware of Ben's attention, whereas she was definitely aware of him. Her eyes never left his face. Isaac had forgotten how good it felt to be the sole focus of someone you admired.

"Seeing Caden so comfortable on a horse has been wonderful." Tabitha's smile turned soft, as if she was picturing the scene. "He's doing things I never imagined he would do."

"It's like that, isn't it?" Isaac remarked, thinking back on his own childhood at the ranch. "I remember when I started riding, I felt like I became another person. As if I was more alive when I was on horseback."

"Yes, exactly." Tabitha nodded with enthusiasm. "I can tell Caden feels that way too. He's just a better, more confident version of himself. It's great. I love that he's able to share something that used to mean a lot to me as a kid as well."

"Have you had a chance to get back on a horse, since you've been here?" Isaac smiled at her, struck with the sudden urge to take her riding with him sometime, if only to confirm what he already suspected about her—that she would ride with surety and grace, the same way she carried herself on her own two feet.

Tabitha returned his smile, her eyes lit with an inner glow. "I've managed to get out a couple of times. Not as much as I'd like, but this program isn't about me. It's about the kids."

"Far as I know, there's no law that says only kids can enjoy the ranch. I think you should ride as much as you want to while you're here," Isaac said. "I could show you the trails sometime."

He didn't know what had come over him. The words he'd been trying to hold back spilled past his lips before he could stop it. Now that he'd offered, he could only stare at Tabitha, torn between hoping she'd shoot him down and praying she wouldn't.

"Really?" She blinked at him, then gave a nod of her head. "I'd like that, Isaac. Thank you."

He realized that he had basically asked her out on a date. And she said yes.

He felt strange realizing what just happened. Not because he regretted suggesting they ride together, but strange for the exact opposite reason. He didn't regret it. And maybe it didn't feel all that strange at all, asking Tabitha out. To his astonishment, it felt rather...good.

He wasn't ready to jump right back into dating or a relationship, but a quiet trek on horseback with Tabitha was something he actually looked forward to. There was even an element of safety to being with her since she would be leaving once the program ended and it was time for her and Caden to return home.

Until then, maybe it wouldn't be so bad pretending he could be a normal, living, breathing human being again. A man who could enjoy the company of a kind, beautiful woman. A friend, even if there was a part of him that stirred with something more than friendship whenever he was near Tabitha.

Caden suddenly reappeared at Tabitha's side with the three cookies he'd fetched. He carefully laid two of them out on the table, one each for his mother and Isaac.

"It's time for the movie, Mom," he announced.

"Oh, right." Tabitha picked up her chocolate chip cookie. "I forgot."

"It's on a big screen outside." Caden turned to Isaac. "I've never seen a movie outside before."

Isaac gave him a smile. "It's been a long time for me too."

"It's exciting, huh?" Tabitha pointed to where the counselors were gathering the kids. "You go on ahead, sweetheart. I'll catch up once I have my cookie."

Caden nodded and then turned to trot after the others.

Tabitha watched him go before turning back to Isaac, her face soft with emotion. "He was never that independent before we came here. This whole program is really helping him develop confidence in every aspect of his life."

Isaac could tell Tabitha was emotional, and to his surprise, her reaction was impacting him too. He wanted to tell her how glad he was that she and her son were finding so much happiness at his family's ranch, but he didn't know how to find the words.

"That's good," he said. "My mother's been working a long time to set this program up, so I'm glad it's going well for you."

Tabitha nodded and took a bite of her cookie. She chewed it, a thoughtful expression in her eyes. "You've been helping her a lot too, right? Vera told me you do all the administrative stuff for the ranch."

"We all help out wherever we can, I suppose." Isaac was uncomfortable with praise. He was just doing what he could for the only thing that mattered to him: the ranch.

"Well, you definitely seem to keep yourself busy." Tabitha's gaze lit on him for a moment before she glanced down at her lap. "I'm glad you made time to come out to the picnic today."

"I am too," he murmured, surprised by how deeply he meant it.

Night began to fall around them. The rest of the picnic attendees had dispersed. The counselors and kids had gone to watch the movie on the projector Beau had set up earlier, and the other Hart brothers had cleaned up and vanished as well.

It was just Tabitha and Isaac and the rustle of the horses in the nearby field.

"Are you going to head over to the movie?" Isaac asked.

Tabitha finished her cookie and brushed the crumbs off her hand. "I think I might swing by the guesthouse first. I need to check on something for one of my work projects, then I'll go get Caden after the movie."

"I can walk you to the guesthouse." Isaac didn't want her to leave him alone. He didn't want the spell to end. "If that's all right."

"Yes, of course."

Tabitha stood up, and together they drifted slowly toward the dirt path that led to the guesthouse.

Standing side by side, her head didn't reach his shoulder.

Isaac was feeling reckless. All the careful work he had put into steering clear of her, all the reasons he had told himself, over and over, about why they were a bad idea, seemed to drift away in the evening breeze.

Logic and reason were banished by his overwhelming desire to be with her.

He didn't want to stay away from her. He wanted to reach out, across the few inches between them, and take her hand.

Soon they were out of sight of the main house. Tabitha took a deep breath, as if she had been waiting for this privacy.

"I've been meaning to tell you." Tabitha's face was shrouded in the gathering darkness, but her words were clear. "I'm sorry if I was a little tense during our last conversation a couple of weeks ago—when you asked about Caden's father. I don't know why I overreacted. It's really not a big deal."

"I should never have asked about your ex," Isaac said. "It was inappropriate, and I am sorry."

Tabitha glanced up at him. "Well, I was worried that it upset you since you never spoke to me after."

She turned away, as if she was embarrassed, but Isaac didn't want her to feel ashamed. In fact, he felt an odd thrill that his absence had bothered her.

"I thought maybe it was best if I kept my distance." Isaac swallowed, aware of how cool his words sounded, even to his own ears. As if he was patronizing them both by denying the clear attraction between them.

Because he knew it was no longer just him. Tabitha felt it, too. There was something special and rare kindling between them. A connection that likely wouldn't end just because she would be leaving in a few more weeks, no matter how much he wanted to convince himself otherwise.

Tabitha seemed like she might say more, but she didn't as they emerged from the woods and onto the small lawn in front of the guesthouse.

They both drew to a stop. Tabitha turned to face him, her uptilted face gleaming under the pale light of the moon.

"I'm sorry," Isaac said. "Sorry for asking about Caden's dad, and I'm also sorry for avoiding you. I wish I hadn't."

He knew the words were dangerous. He knew it was not smart to tell Tabitha how he felt. She was never meant to know how drawn to her he was.

Because he couldn't follow through. He would never be able to date her properly, even if circumstances were different. He couldn't afford to let himself get that close to Tabitha. To risk the hurt of losing her, of letting her into his heart when it still felt so hollow and broken.

He would never want her to fall in love with him. They didn't have a future. Isaac would never be able to give himself entirely to her and Caden.

With the hole in his heart after losing his own child, he couldn't be an instant father. Caden deserved better.

Tabitha did as well. She should have someone who could love her completely. Someone who wouldn't be filled with panic at the thought of losing his family. Someone who didn't have horrific flashbacks to the night when his happiness was burned to ashes in a hospital emergency room.

She stared up at him, and she was silent.

So Isaac said the only words that were in his heart.

"I'm sorry, Tabitha."

He was sorry for the way he had behaved with her before, and he was sorry for everything he might do to hurt her in the future.

He was sorry he couldn't be the man she needed.

Most of all, he was sorry for who he was. Because standing there with Tabitha, Isaac wanted to be anyone else.

CHAPTER 13

Tabitha felt light-headed as she gazed up at Isaac, his gaze solemn and tender, his body heat radiating toward her like a comforting blanket against the chill of the gathering night.

His earnest apology hung between them, along with his unexpected confession that he wished he hadn't been avoiding her these past weeks. Was she reading more into his words than he intended?

Now that it was just the two of them, standing together under the stars, she had the nearly overwhelming urge to reach out to him, to embrace him. To kiss him.

As much as she wanted to act on that urge, she forced her hands to remain at her sides. She forced her thoughts back to her son and the ranch program he was enjoying so much. No way could she put any of Caden's happiness in jeopardy by throwing herself at Isaac Hart.

Especially if he was just trying to be nice.

She didn't have the courage to risk falling in love with a

man she might never see again after the program ended and she and Caden returned home to California.

"There's nothing to apologize for, Isaac. But thank you." Her words were a whisper. "It's fine, really."

Before she was tempted any further to reach her hand up and touch the rigid set of his square jaw or to wrap her arms around the muscular bulk of his body, Tabitha turned and walked to the front steps of the guesthouse's porch. Rather than turning to go, Isaac followed her. She sat down on one of the steps in the long rectangle of light glowing from the window.

Isaac sat beside her. It was as if the previous days of avoidance and awkwardness had evaporated, and now they could simply be. There was no awkwardness now that he was sitting next to her on the porch. She felt an odd sense of ease with him. A familiarity that belied the fact that they had only spoken to each other for a handful of hours during the time she'd been at Hart's Ridge Ranch.

To her own astonishment, Tabitha felt she wanted to tell him everything. She wanted him to know every part of herself. She inhaled a fortifying breath of the fresh country air.

"The only reason I was so startled by your asking about my son's father is because he's not a huge part of Caden's life. We decided to divorce pretty soon after he was born. David's attitude toward Caden was bad, as if Caden and I had disappointed him. We weren't the perfect family he had envisioned, and he had no qualms about letting me know. It was when I realized Caden was starting to realize it too that I knew I couldn't live like that. As for me, I fell out of love with David very quickly."

"That's horrible—for you and for Caden. I'm sorry you

went through that, Tabitha." Isaac's voice was low and intense. He sounded angry at David on their behalf. "You and Caden are not disappointments. You're both wonderful."

Tabitha waved her hand. "It's in the past now." She tilted her head to look at Isaac, her breath catching at how close he was. And yet she was so comfortable with his nearness. She felt she could tell him anything. "I have full custody of Caden, which is my preference. We hardly see David at all."

Tabitha stayed composed. She wasn't going to break down or wallow in sadness over her failed marriage to an unworthy man. Not now, when she was sitting next to a man with a good heart. She knew it. She had only met him a few weeks ago, and it was true they hadn't interacted much, but Tabitha could just tell that every bone in Isaac's body was good and true. And if he loved a woman, his loyalty would have no bounds.

The selfish and greedy part of Tabitha wanted that love. She wanted it with all her soul.

Pain flashed across Isaac's face as he looked at her. Pain for her? Pain for Caden? Isaac's sober, gentle gaze said he felt bad that she had ever endured such heartbreak, and the thought that he sympathized so acutely with her made Tabitha want to cry.

"All children are a blessing," he murmured softly. "Especially one like Caden."

He wasn't just saying that as a cliché statement. Tabitha could tell he believed it. And the way he spoke to Caden, as if Caden was a special person who was unique and worthy of love and attention, only proved how good of a person Isaac was.

"Thank you for saying that." Tabitha bit her lower lip. It seemed odd to be thanking him, but she wanted him to know how grateful she was. "And thank you for being so kind to him earlier."

"It wasn't..." Isaac pulled his hat slowly off his head and let it dangle from his fingers. His dark hair was rumpled and flattened in places but still thick. "I didn't do it as a favor. I like being with Caden. And you."

Tabitha's stomach erupted in butterflies at Isaac's admission. She had sensed something between them, but to hear him say out loud that he liked her company was beyond satisfying.

"I like being with you, too," she said. "These last few weeks, I wasn't sure what to think about you, if I'm being honest. I thought maybe the connection I was feeling with you was only in my head because you were never around."

"No, it wasn't in your head." Isaac shifted closer to her, but his face was etched in a frown. "It's just... complicated."

"I understand." Tabitha nodded, her heart feeling very heavy inside her chest. "Caden and I...well, we're a package deal. I know that's a lot for some men to handle. I suppose I'm a lot to handle for some men too."

"It's not you." Isaac reached out to touch her arm, and Tabitha went still. His hand was strong and warm, yet gentle, on her skin. She looked up at him, and he was staring down at his hand resting lightly on her arm. He didn't withdraw his touch, though his expression seemed tormented. "Tabitha, it's me that's the complicated one. I'm not right for you. I can't be the man you deserve."

"I'm not sure what that means." In that moment, sitting so close to him, Tabitha didn't care who deserved what. She just wanted to be with him. Just the way they were in that moment. She wanted to be with him more than just like this.

"I have a… past." Isaac closed his mouth as if he was physically stopping himself from saying anything else.

Tabitha's heart seized a bit, her mind swirling with all manner of awful scenarios. She couldn't even guess what he meant by having a past. Was he a convicted criminal? Did he have addiction issues?

Normally, a statement like that would throw up major red flags. But this was Isaac, and there was no part of her that could believe he had anything so terrible in his past. A thousand questions churned in her head as she waited for him to say something more. To say anything to assuage her concerns. She was a woman who liked concrete facts, not vague allusions.

But Isaac's solemn gaze had gone from tender to tormented, filled with a fathomless hurt that she didn't dare stir into any darker pain for him. He shifted beside her. His soft touch left her arm as he folded his arms in front of him and inched toward the edge of his seat.

He was getting ready to flee—both the conversation and her.

Abruptly, he stood up. Heaved out a low sigh. "It's late. I should let you go."

Let her go. Why did she get the feeling he was talking about more than simply leaving her for the evening?

Tabitha told herself to stay put on the porch step, but her legs didn't obey. She stood too, turning so that she faced him. "You can talk to me, Isaac. About anything. I'm your friend. I… I care about you."

His tortured look took on a different form, though his expression was no less conflicted. "I'm not ready to talk about it. It's hard to say the words… even now."

She nodded sympathetically. "Okay, then we don't have to

talk about it now. But when you are ready, when you feel you can say the words, just know that I'm here for you."

He stared into her eyes in silence, a tendon working in his jaw. She could almost hear the anguish inside him, the conflict between keeping whatever pain he was feeling bottled up inside him and the need to push it out into the light. But he remained silent, even as his eyes smoldered with an intensity that took her aback.

"Your ex-husband was an idiot," he ground out thickly. He shook his head, reaching up to trace her cheek, his callused fingertips as light as a feather against her skin. "To let you and Caden go the way he did? He was worse than an idiot. If I'd been him, I never would have given you up. I would've done anything to make you both happy, to protect you from any kind of hurt."

Tabitha held perfectly still as his caress lingered on her face and his gaze dropped to her parted lips. Words rose in her throat, demands she yearned to speak aloud. *So, fight for me now. You can have me. I'm willing to be yours.*

She didn't say them, though. She would never know if she would have found the courage to say them.

Because at that same moment, Isaac leaned forward and kissed her.

CHAPTER 14

As he kissed Tabitha, time seemed to slow down until it stopped entirely.

All thoughts and reservations, all his beliefs about why they couldn't be together, evaporated from Isaac's head the moment his lips met hers.

He had to kiss her. Nothing could have stopped him, not even the dark cloud of his lingering grief for Anna.

And it wasn't just due to the force of his own desire. It had been Tabitha's expression when he told her how he felt about her ex's leaving and Isaac's declaration that he would have never been the kind of fool that other man was.

When he pushed away all of his excuses and guilt over betraying Anna's memory and thought simply about Tabitha and Caden, he knew that if he was ever lucky enough to have a family like them, he would do anything to keep them safe and happy. He would hold his family close and never let go, no matter what.

Because he knew what it was like to lose a family you

loved. He lived with that agony every day for the last three years of his life.

It stunned him how the sharp pain of his loss and the grief that clung to him so relentlessly eased while he was holding Tabitha in his arms, kissing her under the stars, and feeling her kiss him back. She tilted her head, and their kiss deepened. Isaac moved his hand up her back and buried it in her unbound hair. He had wondered what it would be like to hold her. To touch her silky dark hair. It was far better than anything he could have imagined.

He knew there was going to be no coming back from this kiss. He would never be able to forget it. No matter how much he wanted to deny his own feelings toward her, the memory of Tabitha in his arms would haunt him for the rest of his days. Somehow, being with her made him feel less broken. She made the shattered pieces of him feel less jagged, as if they could possibly be mended back together again. In such a short time, she was changing him.

He longed to feel whole once more, but he wasn't sure he was ready for all of the new emotions and desires that Tabitha awoke inside him.

He didn't want to consider himself a cowardly man, but what he felt for Tabitha—and her son—scared him for how intensely it made him yearn. For her. For the possibilities of what they could have together. For the chance to feel alive again, to have someone like Tabitha at his side and in his life as a confidante, a friend, a partner. A wife.

A family.

He told himself he was relieved when Tabitha drew in a slow breath and broke their kiss. She pulled away, but only slightly. She reached up, skimming her fingers gently over his jaw. The tender caress and the look of stunned desire in her soft eyes were more than he could bear. On an impulse he couldn't control, he pulled her closer and kissed her once again.

When at last they both drew apart, Tabitha let out a small laugh. "That was, um…"

"Yeah," Isaac murmured, his voice low and rough.

Part of him felt that he should say he was sorry for overstepping when he initiated their kiss, but the way she had returned his passion left him at a loss for words, never mind the ability to put together any kind of apology.

She didn't say anything. She didn't ask what the kiss meant. She stood there in the silent darkness, as if she was just as astonished by what had happened as he was.

Tabitha stepped back, her hands smoothing over her hair as if to reassure herself she was all in one piece. Her gaze turned shy, even a bit awkward now. "It's getting late."

Isaac nodded. "Yes. I've kept you too long."

She didn't deny it. Her fingertips came up to her lips, which still glistened from their kiss under the moonlight. "The movie is probably ending soon. At this point, I should probably just go back for Caden."

"I'll walk you." When she gave him a slight bob of her head, Isaac fell in step beside her. "I hope whatever you wanted to check on for work wasn't urgent."

"No, not at all." She was talking fast, almost as if she was nervous around him now. "I can definitely do it tomorrow."

They walked in silence along the path through the woods. It wasn't awkward, though. It was as if they were both lost in their own thoughts.

Isaac's arm swayed, and his hand bumped into hers. Even that momentary brush of their fingers against each other sent a current of awareness through him. The kiss had been a mistake. Now that he knew the feel of her mouth on his, the taste of her lips, he would only crave it again. If being near Tabitha had been difficult for him before, now, after their kiss, it would be nothing short of torture.

As they neared the end of the path from the guesthouse, the glow from the projector came into sight. The movie viewing was on the other side of the main house from them, but blue light spilled out onto the grass to the side of the house. The distant dialogue rumbled from the speakers.

Isaac slowed and watched Tabitha step forward, and he knew that her next few steps would take them out of the cocoon of the moment they had shared tonight. For his own sake—and for hers too, if he was being honest—it would be best if he took care not to let another moment like that happen between them. Her time at the ranch was only temporary; then they would both go back to their real lives.

She paused a few paces ahead of him and turned her head to look back at him. A question lingered in her eyes. A confusion.

"I have to go to the stables." In truth, he didn't have to do anything in his office except hide. Hide from what had happened between them tonight. From his family before they saw Tabitha and him together. Hide from his own feelings, which right now were the biggest threat to his own sanity. He needed to be alone now.

"Oh," Tabitha said softly. "All right, then. Goodnight, Isaac."

"Goodnight."

She stared at him for a long moment, then turned away, moving across the lawn toward the group of children and parents laughing at something that just happened on the movie screen.

Isaac wanted nothing more than to chase after her and

take her in his arms. In front of everyone. To hold her and tell her that she was his.

But she wasn't his. After the end of the program, she would be gone, and whatever was happening between them would eventually fade into memory. For her, maybe. Not for him.

As Isaac set off to his dark office, his guilt added weight to each step.

He shouldn't have kissed her.

The door to the office shut behind him with a loud *thunk*, and Isaac flicked on the desk lamp, illuminating a harsh circle on the top of the desk. He sank into the old and worn chair.

No, he couldn't bring himself to regret that kiss. It had been too wonderful.

He propped his elbows on the desk and leaned his face in his hands.

He didn't want to fall in love. He hadn't wanted that since Anna and Alice died.

Yet he wanted Tabitha. When he had kissed her, all his concerns about why they couldn't be together had seemed almost inconsequential.

Now that the kiss was over, those concerns were starting to creep back in.

For the first time since Anna had died, Isaac asked himself what she would want him to do.

The thought took his breath away.

What would Anna have wanted for him?

Isaac imagined, as difficult as it was, if he had been the one to die. If it were Anna who survived.

He didn't even have to debate. He knew in his heart that he would have wanted Anna to move on. He would not have wanted her to live forever in a state of grief.

Anna had wanted a family of her own more than anything. She had loved being around people. She was far more extroverted than Isaac. She wouldn't have done well if she had to isolate herself. She also loved teaching. That would have helped her to recover from her grief.

Eventually, Anna would have found someone else to love. It was in her nature, and Isaac wouldn't have wished otherwise. He would have wanted her to find love again. To finally have her family.

Isaac knew Anna would want the same for him. If she had a chance to tell him before she died, she would have. Nearly everyone had echoed this. Anna's own sister had mentioned it to Isaac on the most recent anniversary of her death, and his mother had voiced a similar sentiment.

It was easier said than done, though. Anna might want him to move on, but Isaac wasn't sure he wanted that.

It was too terrifying. The fear of having a family, only to lose it, would never leave him.

He couldn't do that to Tabitha. He already felt bad enough dragging her into his mess as much as he had. He wouldn't drag her further in.

At the end of the day, Isaac knew something that no one else knew. Not his family. Not Anna's family. Not Tabitha.

He was supposed to protect Anna and the unborn baby. To keep them safe from harm.

And he hadn't been able to do that. He had not insisted they go to the hospital as soon as Anna had told him she'd been feeling pain that day. He hadn't called for an ambulance instead of taking her to the hospital in his truck. He had made so many mistakes that day. He had failed Anna. He had failed their unborn daughter.

He couldn't fail anyone he loved ever again.

CHAPTER 15

All morning, Tabitha was a nervous wreck. She was up half the night, tossing and turning, and then she fell asleep just before sunrise and dozed through her alarm.

So she was racing about trying to get Caden dressed and ready, but half her mind was on Isaac.

The kiss had been so unexpected and magical, Tabitha was half convinced she had dreamed the whole thing up.

Only she knew she hadn't. No dream could compare to the way Isaac had held her, as if he was never going to let her go.

In the light of day, though, Tabitha was filled with doubts.

Was she being foolish, letting her heart run away with her good reasoning? Falling in love with Isaac Hart would only lead to trouble. As much as she craved being near him, and now, kissing him, she had Caden to think about. She had herself to think about too, because as lovely as it was spending time with Isaac, when the horsemanship program was over, so were they.

And that ticking clock also didn't diminish the fact that Isaac obviously had things in his past that haunted him.

Things he wasn't ready to open up about with her. Secrets only left her to imagine the worst, and the last thing she wanted was to bring any kind of turmoil or problems into her and Caden's life.

Still, that didn't mean she wasn't totally smitten with the man. Tabitha hadn't ever fallen so hard or so fast for someone. Frankly, she wasn't sure what to do about Isaac Hart now that he had kissed her. As frustrating as his avoidance of her had been before, this new side of him was even more confusing.

Caden could sense her distraction and fussed over his clothes. His socks weren't right, then his little cowboy hat wasn't right, but finally, they got out the door. The others had headed to the first session without them. Tabitha was resigned to being five minutes late, but Caden was visibly upset about it. He probably thought he was missing out.

Tabitha felt bad. One kiss with Isaac and she was already neglecting her son, who was her number-one priority.

She and Caden slipped into the morning session, a review of all the equipment involved with taking care of a horse. To her relief, after a few minutes, Caden settled down.

Tabitha sat in the back with the other parents. She didn't have to stay for the session, but she liked to sit in as often as she could.

Plus, being in the session gave her something to think about besides Isaac. She focused on the counselor and how the information was presented to the kids.

She really wanted to write an article reviewing the program. She had pages and pages of notes, and every day she thought of something else to add.

Of course, it was now looking unlikely that she and Caden would be back next year. Tabitha wanted to return more than anything, but she couldn't imagine coming back and crossing paths with Isaac, depending on how things might end this time. She didn't even know what she would say to him next time they saw each other.

Tabitha looked over at Caden, his eyes bright and alert. He was having so much fun in the program, she worried that he would be devastated when the time came for them to leave Hart's Ridge Ranch. He was obsessed with every facet of ranch life now. It wasn't just the riding. He was fascinated with how the fences and stables were built, and the food the animals ate. He'd even whispered to her one night after evening prayers that he wished they could live on a ranch someday. A ranch with cowboys like Isaac and horses like Bluebell and Lilac.

This ranch had become more than just a temporary escape for Caden and her. And Isaac Hart... well, he had become far more than just a friendly distraction.

Tabitha adjusted in her seat, trying to focus on the session, but her mind refused to settle. Her thoughts wandered to Isaac, to the way his hands had cradled her face when he kissed her, the quiet intensity of his touch. A warmth spread through her chest, and she closed her eyes against the memory. She was already in too deep. She had been from the moment Isaac first smiled at Caden and made her son feel welcome here.

And that was the problem—one kiss, and she was unraveling.

She hadn't meant to let her guard down, but Isaac had a way of slipping past her defenses with a quiet persistence that was almost maddening. It wasn't just his rugged good looks—though those certainly didn't hurt—it was the way he looked at her, like he saw her, really saw her, and wasn't afraid of what he found.

But he was holding her at arm's length emotionally, even after the kiss. Tabitha knew he had his reasons—wounds she couldn't begin to understand. That much was clear from the guarded way he spoke, the way he always seemed to carry the weight of some unseen burden on his broad shoulders.

And yet... she cared. More than she should.

She tried to tell herself that it didn't matter, that this thing with Isaac was fleeting. But deep down, she knew better. The truth gnawed at her: she was falling in love with him. And that terrified her.

Tabitha rubbed her temples, as if the motion could somehow press away the knot of emotions tangled in her chest. This wasn't supposed to happen. She'd come to Wyoming for Caden, not for herself. She hadn't planned to meet a man like Isaac or feel the way she did now—helplessly drawn to him, even though she knew better.

He had warned her with every quiet glance, every hesitant touch, that he wasn't ready to let someone in. And yet, despite his best efforts to keep her at a distance, Tabitha had found herself slipping closer and closer to him.

She knew better than to put her heart on the line for someone who couldn't promise anything in return. She knew the risks. But knowing didn't seem to help. It didn't make her feelings any less real.

She glanced over at Caden, who was now fully engaged, running his hands over the saddle as the counselor showed him how to buckle the straps. Her son looked so at ease here, like he'd belonged on this ranch his whole life. The sight tugged at something deep inside her—a yearning she hadn't expected.

She wanted to belong here too. She wanted this to be more

than just a passing thing, a few fleeting weeks before they packed up and went back to California.

But how could she allow herself to fall for Isaac, knowing how guarded he was? He kept her close one moment, only to push her away the next. The kiss they'd shared had felt like something out of a dream—sweet, slow, full of unspoken promises. Yet she couldn't ignore the way he'd withdrawn after, slipping back into his shell of quiet restraint. As if he regretted it.

Tabitha leaned forward, resting her elbows on her knees. She couldn't afford to be foolish. Not with Caden in the picture. As much as she wanted Isaac, she had learned the hard way that not every man was willing to stay. And falling for someone who seemed determined to keep his heart under lock and key? That was a risk she wasn't sure she could take.

Her stomach twisted as the memory of her ex bubbled to the surface. She had let herself believe in him, in their future together, only to find out how fragile that belief had been. She couldn't make the same mistake again—couldn't put her heart on the line for a man who might not be able to give it back.

And yet, every time she told herself to pull away from Isaac, she only seemed to get drawn deeper.

He was different from anyone she had ever met. His kindness was subtle but steady, a quiet presence that made her feel seen in a way she hadn't in years. He didn't talk much, but when he did, his words mattered. And the way he looked at her—like she was more than just a passing fancy—left her breathless and longing for something she wasn't sure she could have.

Tabitha bit her lip, trying to push those thoughts aside. She had to be practical. The end of the program was coming, and with it, the end of whatever was happening between her and Isaac. That was reality.

California felt impossibly far away from this place—from him. But maybe it wasn't.

The thought came unbidden, slipping into her mind like a whispered temptation. Maybe, if things between her and Isaac continued to grow… maybe they could make this work.

Tabitha bit her lip, weighing the possibilities in her mind. California and Wyoming were far apart, but they weren't worlds away. Flights existed. Road trips existed. If Isaac was willing to try, she would be too.

He had made it clear, in his own way, that he cared. She could see it in the way he was with Caden, the patience he showed her son even when he didn't have to. And that kiss… it hadn't been a mistake, no matter how much either one of them might try to convince themselves otherwise.

A flicker of hope sparked in her chest, cautious but insistent. What if this wasn't just a passing thing? What if Isaac needed time to open up, but they could figure things out together?

What if—just maybe—Caden's dream of living on a ranch didn't have to stay a dream forever? What if he could have a life she'd always dreamed of for him—a life on a ranch, like the one she grew up on, with wide-open skies and horses that felt like friends?

The thought was reckless. It was risky. But it was also beautiful.

Tabitha shifted in her seat, watching as Caden laughed with the other kids, his whole face lit up with joy. She couldn't deny how right this felt—being here, in this place, with these people. With Isaac.

Maybe, just maybe, she thought, they could find a way to make this work.

It was a dangerous hope to cling to. But as she sat there, the sun warming her back and the sound of children's laughter filling the air, Tabitha realized she didn't want to let go of it just yet.

She wasn't ready to walk away from this—not from Isaac, not from the life they could build together, if only he'd let her in.

California didn't feel quite so far away anymore. And if there was even the slightest chance that Isaac might feel the same way... well, maybe the end of the program didn't have to be the end of everything after all.

Tabitha folded her arms, a soft smile curving her lips. Hope was a risky thing, but for the first time in a long while, it felt worth the risk.

CHAPTER 16

After a restless night of little sleep and a frustrating morning spent growling at everyone who dared enter his office, Isaac couldn't put off the inevitable any longer. He had to find Tabitha and speak to her about last night.

He had to find the words to tell her that what happened between them was a mistake. That kiss—the one he could still feel in every fiber of his being today—could not happen again.

For her own good.

For his own sanity, he could never let it happen again.

As he had tossed and turned in bed the night before, he had let himself imagine an alternate universe. One in which he'd told Tabitha he wanted to be with her after they kissed. In that universe, he might be preparing to take her out to supper tonight, or they might be spending the day together riding horses or exploring the ranch.

Isaac had imagined it all. A life with Tabitha and Caden as well. Then he had told himself to banish such thoughts from his head. It wouldn't do to dwell on what could not be.

Isaac shoved his hands into his pockets, scowling at the ground as if the dirt beneath his boots was responsible for his turmoil. The imaginary world he'd let himself slip into last night haunted him. It had been too easy—dangerously easy—to picture a life where he let himself be happy again. A life where he held Tabitha close without hesitation, without guilt. A life where Caden's laughter filled the quiet spaces that once echoed with only grief.

The temptation gnawed at him, even now, in the light of day.

For a moment, he let the memory of that alternate world drift back, uninvited but persistent. He could see it so clearly—Tabitha smiling at him as they rode side by side, her hair catching the breeze. Caden trailing along on a pony, shouting with joy. The three of them sitting around the kitchen table in the evening, eating supper like a family. And at night, Tabitha beside him, a warmth he hadn't known he still craved wrapping around him like a lifeline.

He clenched his jaw, willing the vision to dissipate. It was foolish. Reckless. He couldn't afford to indulge in those kinds of fantasies. Not again. Because the last time he'd dared to believe in something that good, it had shattered right in front of him.

And he knew better now.

Life had a way of reminding you how fragile happiness could be, how easily it slipped through your fingers no matter how hard you tried to hold on. He had learned that lesson the hard way—with Anna, with Alice. He couldn't—wouldn't—put himself in that position again.

And yet, despite every logical reason to stay away, he felt himself being drawn back to Tabitha. Like a moth to a flame, knowing full well the heat could destroy him.

What scared him most was that with every moment he spent near her, every glance they shared, he could feel the ice around his heart begin to thaw. The walls he'd built so carefully, the ones that had kept him safe from the world and from his own pain, were starting to crack.

He hated it. But he also... didn't.

Because as terrifying as the idea of letting someone in again was, the thought of never seeing Tabitha smile at him the way she had last night—that quiet, almost shy way, as if she'd been as stunned by the kiss as he was—felt even worse.

Isaac gritted his teeth, forcing his mind back to the present. He had to tell her the truth. That kiss was a mistake. It couldn't happen again. They were from two different worlds, and what they had—whatever it was—had an expiration date.

She would leave at the end of the program. She had her life in California, and he had his here on the ranch. It was as simple as that.

Except, it wasn't simple.

Because the truth, the one he wasn't ready to admit to anyone—not even himself—was that part of him didn't want her to leave.

That thought stopped him in his tracks, knocking the breath from his lungs. He didn't want her to leave. Not really.

But wanting her to stay was selfish. And if there was one thing he'd promised himself after Anna, it was that he would never be selfish again. He would never put his needs, his desires, above anyone else's.

Especially not Tabitha's.

With a heavy sigh, Isaac dragged a hand down his face. He needed to find the strength to push her away. It was the right thing to do—the only thing to do. But damn if it didn't feel like the hardest thing he'd ever faced.

He straightened his shoulders and set his jaw, knowing what had to be done.

For her sake, for Caden's, and for the fragile sense of control he clung to like a lifeline—he had to let her go. Even if it broke him in the process.

He knew the last morning session would be finishing up before lunch, so around one o'clock he walked slowly toward the main house.

Stepping inside, he saw Tabitha bent over Caden at the long table. A few other ranch guests milled about, the adults clearing plates while their children chattered and cavorted. As soon as Isaac stopped in the dining room doorway, Tabitha's head jerked up, as if she sensed him there. A warm smile spread slowly over her lips before her bright eyes connected with his grim stare.

Their eyes met for only a second, but in that moment, Tabitha seemed to understand everything. She knew Isaac had something to tell her, and she knew it was going to be a difficult conversation. Isaac was once again overwhelmed with how easy it was for her to read him. She seemed to see so much more than others when she looked at his face.

Tabitha looked back down at Caden and began to help him out of his seat. Isaac was about to drift back into the hallway to wait there, but then Caden caught sight of him.

"Isaac!" The boy called out to him, and Isaac couldn't ignore him.

He smiled as Caden walked toward him.

"Hi, Caden." Isaac crouched down on his haunches. "You gonna ride later this afternoon?"

"Yup." Caden nodded with excitement.

Tabitha drifted over, smiling at her son even though her wary gaze remained on Isaac. "Caden, please go wash your hands at the sink." Her voice was soft but firm. "Miss Donna's in the kitchen. She'll help you get cleaned up."

Caden whirled around and marched into the kitchen. Tabitha stayed behind, so it was just her and Isaac in the empty dining room.

Isaac took a quick mental inventory of his family members to ensure he and Tabitha would be alone for the next few minutes. His mother would be down at the paddock with the riders, Liam was teaching a lesson with Beau and Diane, and both Jacob and his dad had just entered the stables when Isaac left. That about covered the most likely suspects for eavesdropping. Mateo was probably out, but even if Mateo overheard something, he would never tell.

"We should talk," Isaac said.

Tabitha nodded; the movement was stiff. Isaac looked closer at her face and wondered if she'd gotten much sleep last night either. Her cheeks seemed a bit pale, and she had purple shadows beneath her luminous eyes. Her dark hair was pulled back in a messy ponytail. To him, she was as beautiful as ever, despite that she was clearly exhausted.

Isaac walked to the table and sat down. Tabitha sat across from him. It was good to have the thick wooden table between them. Otherwise, he might be too tempted to reach out and pull her into his arms again. Even though he'd come to say what he did, every bone in his body longed for the opposite. He wanted to be closer to her, to give her comfort.

Tabitha sat with her shoulders back, her hands clasping what looked to be a mug of cold coffee.

Isaac awkwardly cleared his throat. "I'm, ah… I wanted to say that I'm sorry. About last night."

Tabitha's face remained schooled as the words hit her. She inhaled a slow breath, then quietly let it go. She slowly nodded but offered no other reaction. It was as if she was expecting this kind of conversation.

"I never should have kissed you." Isaac couldn't call it a mistake. He couldn't say that out loud now, to her face. He couldn't watch her silently absorb that blow on top of everything else. Especially when it hadn't felt like a mistake. Not to him.

"If you recall, I kissed you, too." Tabitha's voice was husky and soft, but steady. "I didn't expect to be apologizing today, but if our kiss made a complicated situation even more tangled for you, then I am sorry. I'm sorry if I misread the situation."

Isaac wanted to kick himself now. "Tabitha, you didn't misread anything."

Tabitha's eyes stayed locked on his, unflinching. "Then what's this conversation about, Isaac?" she asked, her voice calm but edged with a frustration she was clearly trying to hold back.

Isaac dragged a hand through his hair, searching for words that didn't feel like stones in his mouth. "It's just… I think it'd be best if we kept some distance. For both of us."

Her lips pressed into a thin line, and she gave a small, humorless laugh. "Distance." She rolled the word on her tongue as if testing its weight, her gaze flicking toward the window, out to where the ranch stretched endlessly under the sun. "This is a big place. Plenty of space for distance."

Isaac winced, her sharpness hitting harder than he expected. She wasn't yelling or making a scene—she was far too composed for that—but the coolness in her voice cut deeper than anger would have.

"Distance hasn't been working very well for us so far," she added.

Isaac felt his defenses rising, but before he could respond, Tabitha leaned forward slightly, her voice soft but edged with something sharper. "What is this really about, Isaac? Last night, it felt like things had shifted between us. I thought maybe... maybe you weren't going to keep doing this—pushing me away every time we get close. Avoiding me. But here you are, doing it all over again."

"I'm not avoiding you," Isaac muttered, straightening in his chair. "I'm sitting right here, aren't I?"

She exhaled sharply through her nose and gave him a flat look. "You know exactly what I mean."

Isaac opened his mouth, then closed it again, feeling the weight of her gaze pressing on him. He could argue with her, but she wasn't wrong. Not really.

Tabitha's expression softened, though her frustration was still palpable. "Why don't you just talk to me, Isaac? Whatever it is you're carrying—whatever's making you think you have to keep me at arm's length—just say it. I'm not going to judge you. I just want to understand."

Isaac stared at her, every muscle in his body tightening as the words sat heavy on his tongue. He wanted to tell her. He wanted to lay it all out—the guilt, the fear, the way every moment with her and Caden made him feel like he was standing at the edge of a cliff with no way back.

He wanted to tell her how much he'd failed Anna and Alice. How every night since their deaths had been haunted by what-ifs and regrets that gnawed at him until he felt like he was unraveling from the inside out.

But how could he say any of that without breaking? And if he broke now—in front of Tabitha, in the middle of the family dining room—how could he ever put himself back together again?

His pride kept him locked in place, the walls around him standing firm, even as he could feel them cracking under the weight of everything he wasn't saying.

"I can't," he whispered, almost to himself.

Tabitha's expression didn't falter, but there was a flicker of disappointment in her eyes that twisted in his gut. "You mean you won't," she said quietly, as if that distinction made all the difference.

Isaac rubbed the back of his neck, frustration and guilt warring inside him. "Look, I don't want to make things harder for you. Or for Caden." He shifted in his seat, glancing down at the worn wood of the table as if it might give him an answer. "If it's too much having me around, I can leave for the rest of the program. I've got friends nearby I can stay with."

Tabitha's jaw tightened, and for a moment, he thought she might take him up on the offer. But instead, she drew a deep breath and sat back in her chair, folding her arms over her chest.

"That's not necessary," she said, her tone clipped but steady. "We're both adults. We can handle this."

Isaac studied her, trying to gauge if she really meant what she was saying or if she was just trying to save face. Her expression gave nothing away except quiet resolve. He nodded, though his chest felt like it was being squeezed in a vise.

Tabitha gave him a small, tight smile, the kind that didn't reach her eyes. "We'll forget about the kiss. Move on. Be friends."

Friends. The word grated against him, but he forced himself to nod again. "Yeah. Friends."

It was what he'd wanted, wasn't it? A way to put the kiss behind them, to restore some sense of order and control.

Right now, all it felt like was a loss.

Silence stretched between them, heavy and awkward, but Tabitha made no move to leave. Isaac's hand curled into a fist on the table, the wood cool beneath his skin. He wanted to say something more, to reach across the table and tell her he didn't really want distance, that forgetting the kiss felt impossible. But the words refused to come.

Finally, Tabitha exhaled softly and stood, brushing her hands down her jeans as if wiping away the last traces of their conversation. "I should check on Caden."

Isaac stood too, his legs feeling heavier than they should. "Yeah. Of course."

She gave him a polite smile that felt like a knife twisting in his chest. "Thanks for the talk, Isaac. It's good to know at least something about how you feel."

And then she was gone, leaving him standing alone in the dining room, feeling colder than he had before.

Isaac sat back down heavily, elbows on the table, and ran both hands over his face. He had gotten what he needed—distance, space to keep himself from slipping any further into feelings he didn't know how to handle. But all he could think about now was the aching weight in his chest, the sense that he had just let something precious slip through his fingers.

He told himself it was for the best. It was the right thing to do.

So why did it feel so wrong?

CHAPTER 17

Tabitha had work to do, but she put it off. She opted instead to spend the whole day watching Caden ride and attend his sessions. She needed to see how happy her son was. She needed to remind herself that he was thriving.

After all, Caden was the reason she didn't rush back to the guesthouse, throw all their things into the car, grab Caden, and drive away, back to her quiet life in California.

The conversation with Isaac had been awful. There was so much he wasn't saying—she knew it. Isaac was a man with hidden depths and, obviously, hidden pain.

Part of her had wanted to demand he tell her what was holding him back. She wanted specifics. Deep down, part of her wondered if some of his reluctance to open up was the fact that she was a single mother to a child who had special needs. She had dismissed that idea at first, and certainly Isaac's behavior with Caden gave her no reason to doubt him where her son was concerned. But Isaac's refusal to open up to her left her to imagine every possible excuse. She wouldn't hold it against him if the idea of Caden and her was simply just too much for him. She just wanted to hear the truth from him.

But what was the point now? As he said, their kiss was a one-time thing. It was behind them now, where he clearly wanted it to stay.

She couldn't pretend she hadn't seen it coming. As soon as she saw his grave face in the dining room, she knew. She had figured the conversation would go the way it had, and yet it had still felt like a dagger in her chest.

As Tabitha watched Caden laugh atop his trotting horse, she leaned against the paddock fence and forced herself to smile. Her son was happy. That was the most important thing.

A small voice tickled the back of her head: *Does that mean you don't get to be happy?*

Tabitha dismissed the question. She was happy. She had Caden and a good job that she enjoyed. She had been completely content with her life.

Until she met Isaac. Until she saw what more there could be for her.

Tabitha had almost cried in the kitchen after hurrying away from the table and Isaac. She had been shocked by the wave of emotion, the swelling sorrow in her throat.

Only her pride kept her composed. She was tougher than that. She had survived a divorce and years of single motherhood. She wasn't going to let a handsome and emotionally closed-off cowboy reduce her to tears.

So, she had kept her head held high and her smile pasted in place in front of Caden and the counselor who'd been helping him wash up after lunch. Tabitha was sure Donna sensed her upset, but the older woman only touched her shoulder before going about her business in the kitchen.

Tabitha thought back on how she'd suggested to Isaac that

they could simply be friends going forward. She'd meant it, only because the idea of severing all connection to him was too much to bear. Still, she had no idea how friendship was going to work with him, since she fully assumed Isaac would immediately go back to avoiding and ignoring her.

She wanted to hate him. She wanted to dismiss him as an uncaring jerk who was being purposely evasive, if for no other reason than to avoid having to tell her an uncomfortable truth that might somehow paint him in a bad light.

The thing was, she knew he wasn't like that. Whatever was holding Isaac back, whatever secrets lurked in his past, they were real, and they were painful for him.

So, she couldn't hate him. In fact, Tabitha had felt the opposite when she'd been seated across from him at the table earlier. She had looked into his earnest gaze, as they both agreed to be friends and nothing more, and she had thought to herself that this might be the only man she could ever love.

After Caden was finished riding, Tabitha joined the kids and counselors for a nature walk. It calmed her to be with Caden and to think about simpler things, like looking for specific types of plants and small animals.

By the time they were back at the guesthouse enjoying a quiet supper with the other families and not at the main house, Tabitha was feeling much better. She would sleep well tonight and wake up the next day ready to focus on Caden and on being politely friendly toward Isaac—and to forget everything that had happened between them.

No, forgetting wouldn't be possible. She could just pretend like she had forgotten. That was the best she could manage.

As she prepared for bed, Tabitha told herself that, in a way, she was grateful. Isaac had nipped things in the bud before she had the chance to risk any more of her heart on him. She was grateful, but she was also sad. Luckily, due to her lack of sleep the night before and her day of overthinking and walking around the ranch, she was exhausted. She fell asleep almost as soon as her head hit her pillow, as if her body knew she needed to drown her thoughts in a deep slumber.

The next morning, she was determined to act more like herself. Cindy had cast plenty of suspicious glances her way the day before, as if the other mom sensed something was up, and Tabitha wasn't sure she could use a bad night's sleep as an excuse anymore.

So, Tabitha and Caden were dressed and in the kitchen bright and early. While Caden ate his pancakes, Tabitha made eggs and bacon for everyone else.

When Cindy came down, Tabitha chatted with her friend about the plan for the day. Tabitha sometimes felt her tone was a little too cheerful and maybe her eyes were too bright, but all in all, she thought she gave a good performance.

She had to. As much as it might be nice to confide in someone, if Cindy found out that Tabitha and Isaac had kissed, Cindy would want to know details. She would also hopelessly romanticize the whole thing. Cindy had already told Tabitha she had to come visit Austin and meet some of Cindy's available friends, as she was determined to set Tabitha up with someone. If Cindy knew Tabitha had a spark with Isaac, her new friend would be relentless.

She would also stare at Tabitha and Isaac every time they were in a room together, which Tabitha knew she couldn't bear. It would be too much. Cindy had to remain in the dark.

After dropping Caden off with the counselors at the main house, Tabitha decided to head back to the guesthouse and take care of the work she had put off the day before.

Vera stopped her on the way out.

"Tabitha, you're heading over to the guesthouse?" Vera held out a bridle. "Could you drop this off in the stables for me? Just hang it on the row of hooks just inside the door."

"Of course." Tabitha took the bridle from Vera.

"I just repaired it last night, and I think Beau will need it today." Vera looked over her shoulder as one of the counselors called for her. "Thank you again."

Tabitha smiled as Vera dashed off. The woman was giving everything to the program, and Tabitha admired that. Vera Hart was the reason it had been such a success, no matter how much Vera tried to push the praise onto the counselors and Donna. It was Vera's concept, her organization, and her dedication that made the program so special. Tabitha only hoped to have Vera's energy when she was that age.

It probably helped that Vera had such an amazing and supportive husband in Tom Hart.

They both were lucky to have each other and to have enjoyed such a long and happy marriage. With most of their sons paired off and either engaged or thinking about it, before long Vera and Tom would be welcoming grandchildren into their idyllic family circle.

Tabitha shook off her envy as she headed to the stables. She couldn't go through the rest of her life wondering how it would be different if she had a partner. She had to find happiness in the life she had. Meeting Isaac had complicated that now, but Tabitha was sure that, with time, she could find her old sense of peace.

She just worried that maybe she didn't want to find that peace again. Maybe a part of her, a wild and reckless part, liked how Isaac had disrupted her equilibrium so thoroughly.

The doors to the stable were open, and Tabitha stepped into the wide center aisle. It was quiet, except for the stirring of a few of the horses. Tabitha hung up the bridle and wandered past a few of the stalls, admiring some of the animals. She stopped across from a stall holding a lovely mare. The label claimed her name was Maeve.

The horse stiffened and scuffed her hooves at the sight of Tabitha. Maeve pulled her long neck back, and Tabitha could see the whites of her eyes. The horse was skittish and likely untrained. She had to be one of the new ones that Beau and Diane were working with.

Tabitha clucked her tongue, trying to offer the horse a comforting sound, but she didn't get closer. A mare like Maeve was not for petting. Tabitha had learned early about proper caution around horses.

She was turning back when a door to her right swung open. Tabitha went perfectly still as Isaac appeared, a sheaf of papers in his hand. He froze when he saw her.

Of course. This was his office, where he retreated so often.

Tabitha pulsed with embarrassment. He would think she had sought him out.

"I was just putting a bridle back." Tabitha pointed at the row of hooks. "For your mom."

Isaac, as if in a daze, slowly swung his head to where she indicated, then back to her. "Oh."

"I wasn't looking for you or anything," Tabitha blurted out.

She blushed at how pathetic and defensive she sounded, but Isaac just smiled. "I didn't think you were."

His eyes were sparkling with mild amusement, and that put Tabitha at ease. She chuckled and shrugged. "I guess I could look for you if I wanted, though, since we're friends now, right?"

Her words edged dangerously close to being flirtatious, but she couldn't stop herself.

Isaac didn't seem to mind. "Exactly. And if you ever are looking for me, this would be the best place to come." He held up his papers. "I was just going through some bills of sale."

"Ah, I won't keep you, then."

Tabitha started to walk past him, but Isaac shook his head.

"Actually, I'm done for today." He ducked back into the office and put the papers on a wide desk, then emerged and stood next to Tabitha.

This was not at all part of the plan, but Tabitha couldn't find a reason to leave. Not when he was looking so tall and handsome.

Or rather, she could think of plenty of reasons. Her unfinished work project waiting back at the guesthouse. Her vow to be mature and guard her heart. The fact that she could never have Isaac, not in the way she wanted.

Those were all the reasons to make an excuse and depart. She just didn't want to think about any of those reasons.

"I was just looking at that mare, Maeve." Tabitha nodded toward the stall. "Is she new to the ranch?"

He nodded, his dark brown cowboy hat dipping with the movement. "We bought her last month," Isaac said. "She's beautiful, but pretty much totally untrained. And skittish. That's why we have to keep her separate most of the time."

"I saw Diane training the other day," Tabitha said. "She's very good. She has the touch that ranchers are always talking about."

"Definitely." Isaac stepped closer. "What about you? Do you feel like you've been able to get back in touch with your ranching roots yet?"

Tabitha laughed and shook her head. "Not as much as I'd like."

"That offer to come riding with me still stands," he said. "Want to go for a short ride?"

She practically gulped. "Right now?"

He nodded. His eyes bore into hers, showing how earnest his invitation was. "I'll show you the ranch."

"I don't want to pull you away from your work." Tabitha felt she had to put up some sort of resistance. She had to give them both a chance to think better of this plan, even though she desperately wanted to go on this ride.

"I'm at a good break, and I could use some fresh air and sunshine."

Every fiber of her being wanted to leap at his offer, but she was still stinging after yesterday, so she was sure her expression showed her wariness. "If you're sure..."

"Come with me," he said, then started walking down the aisle of the stable. "I have just the horse for you."

Tabitha followed along, anxious yet elated at the chance to spend time with him—and to be able to do it on horseback, one of her favorite things in the world. He stopped in front of a stable and placed his hand on the wood-planked door. Tabitha looked in and saw a tall, beautiful roan mare pushing her nose against Isaac's shoulder.

"This is Sunday," Isaac said. "She's got a good temperament, but she isn't lazy. I'm sure she'd love to show you around the property today."

He grinned at Tabitha, and she knew she was totally helpless to refuse. Her hands were already itching to put a saddle on Sunday and swing herself up into it.

"Yes," Tabitha said. "Yes, I'd like that."

CHAPTER 18

It was nothing, just something friends might do. That's what Isaac told himself as he showed Tabitha where the saddles and tack were kept.

In truth, he knew he was standing much closer than necessary as he placed the bridle into her hands and led her back toward Sunday's stall.

He had just been so happy to see her, relieved when she'd been nice to him, instead of cold as he had feared—and justly deserved—that he couldn't resist inviting her on the ride he'd promised days ago.

It was just a ride. That's what he told himself. It was a way to break the ice between them again, a way to demonstrate that he intended to make the effort to be a friend to her, even if he wasn't capable of giving her more than that.

He kept sneaking glances at Tabitha as she saddled up Sunday with expert hands. She was smiling to herself as she moved, as if lost in a happy memory.

"Did you ride often as a kid?" Isaac asked.

"Yes," Tabitha said. "Every chance I could get."

She ran a gentle hand over the horse's smooth neck and murmured something in the mare's ear.

While she got acquainted with Sunday, Isaac led his own horse, Ranger, from his stall. Isaac rode Ranger often, but usually on solitary rides, and normally more for the horse's sake than his own. Ranger needed exercise, so Isaac gave it to him. Riding, like so many activities that he once loved, had lost a lot of its joy in recent years.

But saddling up Ranger while Tabitha tightened the stirrups on Sunday made Isaac feel a bit like his old self again. He felt that long-dead buzz of adrenaline at the thought of galloping across a distant field on the ranch. Riding to a secluded spot, far away from watching eyes. Somewhere he and Tabitha could just be themselves.

When they were both ready, they led their horses out the back of the stable. Tabitha was dressed in jeans and a long-sleeved, button-down shirt, as well as boots. Common enough attire for a day on the ranch, and he was glad for that now. It was perfect for taking off on horseback.

As they walked their mounts outside, it felt as if the universe was conspiring to give them the privacy they needed to get their relationship—their friendship, he corrected himself—back on track. Behind the stable, there was no one around. No brothers to throw incredulous looks their way. No sign of Vera or Tom nearby. No nosy coworkers or counselors asking where they were going.

"I was never a hardcore competitive rider, just so you know," Tabitha said as she stepped into a stirrup then swung her other leg smoothly over Sunday's saddled back. "I never did barrel races or shows or anything like that."

Isaac cocked his head and grinned at her. "Are you nervous?"

"No, not nervous." Tabitha's eyes sparkled with glee and something secretive and mischievous. "Just want you to have the right expectations."

"Ah, consider me warned." Isaac grinned, realizing he was flirting with her. It was impossible not to be drawn to Tabitha, though. Especially when she was glowing with excitement, her dark hair infused with copper light under the afternoon sun, and her cheeks flushed with color that seemed to bloom a bit brighter as she held his mesmerized gaze. "All right, Ms. Young, let's see what you've got, then."

Tabitha's eyes crinkled at the corners as she smiled at him in return. Her body relaxed into a perfect riding position as she nudged Sunday into movement, as if woman and horse were one.

Isaac mounted up as well and pushed Ranger into a trot to catch up.

They guided the horses around the edge of a fence and into an open field.

Isaac nodded at the swell of the hill. "Ready for a gallop?"

Instead of answering with words, Tabitha let out a laugh and urged Sunday into a canter. Isaac was only a beat behind her.

As they rode up the green hill, Isaac felt lighter and freer than he had in years. This was what it had felt like to ride when he was young, and his entire life was in front of him. The fact that his horse was trailing close behind Tabitha's, with the beauty of Hart's Ridge Ranch spread out all around them only made the moment more perfect. It was surreal, in fact, making him appreciate his family's land in a whole new light.

The horses rode atop the flat above the hill and then down the other side. Now they were well out of sight from the ranch buildings. Tabitha slowed Sunday, giving Isaac and Ranger a chance to catch up and ride alongside them. All the words that had been exchanged between them, all the ways Isaac had fumbled when it came to Tabitha, seemed to fall away out here in the open pasture with the jagged peaks of the mountains a hazy hint in the distance.

Tabitha let Sunday slow to a walk, then swiveled her head to look at Isaac.

Her cheeks were slightly flushed, and her dark hair hung in tangled waves down her back. Her shoulders were loose and relaxed, and there was a lightness to her, as if she, too, had shed years of stress in the mad gallop over the hill.

Isaac's breath caught in his throat as he rode beside her. She had never looked so lovely.

His resolve to not reach out and touch her, to not kiss her —to stay friends and nothing more—seemed to crumble.

"That was amazing!" Tabitha took a deep breath, her chest rising and falling.

"It was." Isaac wanted to tell her that she was amazing too. It took nearly biting his tongue in half to keep the thought to himself.

"Well, where next?" Tabitha asked. "You promised a tour, so show me the rest of the ranch."

Isaac nodded toward the dense growth of woods ahead. "There's a path up to a higher pasture through there. If you don't mind a long ride."

"No, I don't mind." Tabitha pulled the reins to point Sunday toward the path. "Caden will be in sessions for the next couple of hours, so I can do a longer ride."

So they rode up through the woods, the horses picking their way over rocks and shaded, dusty paths.

Tabitha told Isaac more about her family's ranch, and the

trips she would take with her father to pick up a new horse or supplies. Isaac talked about how much he and his brothers always wanted to help out with the ranch as soon as they were old enough.

"You never thought about doing anything else?" Tabitha asked. "Going to college or moving to a city?"

"Not me. Not Jacob either. When we were kids, we basically had the same mind." Isaac shrugged. "No other job seemed half as good as being a rancher."

"With a ranch like this, I can see why you thought that." Tabitha looked over at him, growing bold in the quiet of nature, far away from everyone else. "Has it ever gotten hard to be constantly surrounded by family?"

"Yes," Isaac said. "Especially since everyone in my family has an opinion."

Tabitha laughed. "I've noticed that."

"You get used to it," Isaac said. "And at the end of the day, there are more pros than cons to living near family."

"I believe that." Tabitha's eyes softened wistfully, as if she were imagining how nice it would be to have a built-in support system like he had. "My siblings are all spread out now. I think we missed our chance to all settle down on a family ranch together."

Isaac tried his best not to picture Tabitha and Caden being part of life at Hart's Ridge Ranch. He'd gotten accustomed to seeing them both around the place, from the frequent meals at the main house, to all the time they spent around the paddocks and horses. Even though it wasn't their home—they weren't part of his family—it was going to be strange not seeing them every day. Worse than strange, he realized. It was going to seem a lot less lively, less colorful, without Tabitha and her son at the ranch.

With the subject of family so close at hand, it was also impossible not to think about Anna and Alice. Part of him wanted to confide in Tabitha now, to do something to clear the air between them and assure her that she hadn't done anything wrong to deserve the way he'd shut her out after their kiss.

Isaac took a fortifying breath, urging himself to force the words out before he could change his mind. He might have, but then the woods cleared up ahead, and Tabitha gasped aloud at the painted colors of the vast afternoon sky opening up above them.

"Oh, my goodness," she whispered, clearly awestruck.

They emerged into the high pasture, onto a patch of flat grass that offered one of the most stunning views down into the valleys and out to the distant mountains.

"It's absolutely beautiful," Tabitha breathed.

Isaac looked at her face, glowing in her awe. The bright afternoon light seemed to illuminate her pale skin and set her dark hair afire from within.

Tabitha turned to him, her hazel eyes huge in her face. Tears glistened in the warm sunlight. "That stunning sky, that breathtaking landscape beneath it. It's a reminder of just how small we all are, don't you agree?"

"And that's a good thing? To feel how small we are?" Isaac furrowed his brow.

"Yes," Tabitha said. "It's comforting sometimes to know that all our pain and struggles are only temporary. Life continues all around us. It always will, even after we're gone."

Isaac still didn't see how that was comforting.

Tabitha saw his confusion, and she fidgeted with the leather reins as she tried to think of a way to explain.

"It's a reminder that I shouldn't worry so much about

everything that doesn't go the way I plan, or the way I wish it could," Tabitha said. "Instead, I should appreciate the good things and savor the time I do have. Because it's a big world, and the days may feel long, but the years are short."

Understanding dawned on Isaac. For Tabitha, every day was filled with some sort of stress. She worried about Caden and about his development and making sure he was okay. She had to support him herself, so she probably worried about keeping her job. From sunup to sundown, she was nonstop. Every day probably felt like a marathon to her. And yet years flew by. She probably was thinking that she needed to savor her time with Caden, even when things were stressful.

As for Isaac, he was a temporary source of pain for her. She would get over him before long. Her life would go on, as it should, after she left Hart's Ridge Ranch.

Isaac would have loved to join her in her philosophy. He would have liked to push aside his personal pain and grief and enjoy what he did have. Only he had nothing. Tabitha had her son and her job and her friends. Isaac had his family, but he barely knew how to be with them anymore; they all seemed so disappointed in him and how his grief had altered his personality.

"The years are short." Isaac nodded his agreement. "I bet time moves even faster when you have a child."

"It does." Tabitha nodded, and the horses started walking again, meandering somewhat aimlessly through the grass. It was fine with Isaac if they let the horses roam for a while. He was in no hurry to get back. Tabitha didn't seem to be either. "Sometimes it feels like just yesterday I was pregnant with Caden, still waiting to meet him."

Isaac pictured Tabitha pregnant, her hand on a swollen

belly, her soft and knowing smile as she dreamed of the life inside her.

Pain cut through him as he recalled the pure joy he and Anna had felt when they were expecting. He had wanted a child so badly.

For the first time, Isaac imagined what his life would be like if Anna had been the only one to pass away, leaving him to care for Alice on his own. The night they both died had seemed so final. Isaac had never bothered with hypotheticals. But now he did.

Being a single father would have been hard, but his parents and brothers would have helped. And he would have a little girl, a daughter. She would be three, going on four. Maybe she would have blonde hair, like Anna did.

Everything would be different. Isaac would still have grieved, but he would have had something—someone—to live for. His daughter would have given him purpose and joy. She would have pulled him out of his grief.

Isaac glanced over at Tabitha and wondered if she and Caden could do the same. If they could pull him out of his solitude.

He dismissed the thought just as quickly. It felt like a betrayal of the family he had lost, to think that anyone could somehow replace them. Worse still, it wasn't fair to Tabitha to put that kind of burden on her and her son.

Isaac's morose thoughts only refortified his reasoning for keeping things casual with her. Until he could make room in his heart for Tabitha on his own, he wasn't ready to pursue anything deeper than friendship with her.

At long last, they circled back to the path.

"Ready to head back?" Isaac didn't want to end their time together, but he knew the ride couldn't last forever.

Tabitha sighed, as if she was regretting the imminent end to the ride as much as he was. "Yes, I suppose we better."

They rode back down the trail, talking easily about the program, Caden, and Isaac's work. Tabitha even offered some advice on improving the ranch's website, a welcome gesture given that web design was her specialty. Their conversation felt natural now—no tension, no awkward silences. They enjoyed each other's company the way real friends would.

Which was good. That's what they'd agreed to be. Friends.

And yet, as the ranch came back into view and the afternoon sun cast long shadows over the fields, the word felt more like a warning than a promise. Isaac knew he should feel relieved, grateful even, that they had found a way to ease back into safe territory.

But instead, it felt like trying to rope a wild horse—forcing something that was never meant to stay contained.

And deep down, Isaac knew that pretending they could be just friends might turn out to be the biggest mistake of all.

CHAPTER 19

Tabitha had loved every second of the ride with Isaac—the freedom of galloping over the green pasture, the comfort she felt as they rode up to the stunning view that awaited them.

And Isaac. She would only be lying to herself if she said part of the joy wasn't in the man with whom she'd shared her afternoon.

They made it back to the stables, and Isaac dismounted first. When Tabitha swung her leg over the side of Sunday, she thought she saw Isaac move as if he might have intended to help her down, but he held himself in place instead. It was fine. They were just friends, after all. The ride hadn't been a romantic date, no matter how pleasant it had been. Besides, she was more than capable of dismounting by herself.

Even so, it felt like the whole ride had been a study in mixed signals. Isaac had flirted with her. He smiled at her and asked her thoughtful questions. He'd been a perfect gentleman and an enjoyable companion, but she couldn't let herself get carried away simply because they'd shared a wonderful couple of hours together. He had made himself pretty clear that he didn't want to date her. He wanted to be friends.

To be honest, she had said the same thing to him, but only because her pride had been injured to realize their kiss hadn't meant as much to him as it had to her.

Tabitha took her time brushing down Sunday, and Isaac seemed willing to linger in the stables as well. After some time, she stepped out of the horse's stall. Caden would be starting his next session soon, a riding instruction, and Tabitha loved to watch. He liked it, too. He always asked her at the end of each day if she had seen what he had done in the paddock. He liked to report a play-by-play for her of every little thing he and his horse had done.

Tabitha stopped in the center of the aisle. Isaac stood a few feet away, his hat in his hands.

The top of his hair was mussed, some of the thick, dark strands stuck flat to his forehead. She longed to reach up and run her fingers through it.

"Thank you for today," she said. It was difficult to express how much the last few hours had meant to her. "That ride was… amazing."

He gave her a nod, his dark gaze rooted on her. "No need to thank me."

"No, I do have to." Tabitha waved her hand, trying to find the words.

She knew what she wanted to say to him, but she was afraid to say the words that popped into her head. That she loved spending time with him. That she wished they had more time left, so they could start over again, try getting to know each other better without the missteps they'd taken along the way.

That she hoped he would eventually realize that he could trust her with the pain that haunted him.

That maybe, somehow, she could help him through it—even if all he wanted from her was friendship.

All those words and more stayed lodged in her throat as she held his gaze, reluctant to end their perfect afternoon yet knowing she had to.

She offered him a faint smile. "Just... thank you, Isaac."

Isaac accepted her thanks this time with a gracious nod.

"I should go now." Tabitha spoke the sentence quietly, but she didn't move.

Instead, her boots stayed rooted to the stable floor as Isaac took a step closer to her. She held her breath. He was close. Close enough to kiss.

She thought they might, but she wouldn't be the one to initiate. She was too hesitant and too confused.

He reached up and placed his hand on her cheek. His fingers were warm and callused against her skin, but his touch was gentle.

With a dark frown, he dropped his hand back to his side. He put his hat on his head and tugged it lower over his forehead. "Yes, you should go."

Tabitha swallowed, unsure how to move at all now. It wasn't until he pivoted away from her and strode back into the shadows of the stables that she found the will to set her own feet into motion. Turning on her heel, she nearly ran from the stables.

She didn't know what he wanted from her. She wasn't sure what she wanted from him either, but it wasn't the emotional roller coaster of whatever limbo in which he'd placed them.

A half hour later, Tabitha was still reeling in her confusion where she sat on the back porch of the main house to watch

Caden at his lesson. The other children's parents were watching down near the paddock, but Tabitha could see well enough from where she was. She wasn't in the mood to chat.

She watched Caden laugh out loud as he bounced on the back of his cantering horse. The sound of her son's laughter brought an automatic smile to her face.

The truth was it had been a good day. Even though she was frustrated with Isaac's mixed signals, the ride up to the top pasture had been so worth it. It had felt so good to be on a horse again, to gallop. It had been freeing.

She probably wouldn't get the chance to repeat it. Isaac was unpredictable. He might show up the next day smiling at her, or he might turn into a ghost for two weeks.

Tabitha let out a long sigh. Would she ever be able to make sense of the man and his shifting moods? She leaned back in the wooden Adirondack chair. It was golden hour—the time of day in the late afternoon when everything seemed lovely and dipped in a warm, shimmery light.

"Lovely, isn't it?"

Tabitha turned at the sudden voice to see Elizabeth Grayson standing in the doorframe. Jacob's fiancée pushed open the screen door and crossed the porch. "Mind if I join you?"

"Of course not." Tabitha gestured to the chair next to her. Elizabeth certainly had more claim to the ranch than Tabitha did, but Tabitha had learned that it was in Elizabeth's nature to be polite. The auburn-haired woman was quiet and gentle and had a heart of gold.

Elizabeth folded her lean body into the chair with natural grace. "How was your day?"

"It was good." Tabitha hesitated, but only for a moment. There was no point denying where she had been—or with whom. Her ride with Isaac wasn't a secret she needed to keep, and surely someone must have seen them, even from a distance. "I went for a ride up to the woods to see the view... with Isaac. We just got back a few minutes ago."

"Beautiful day for that," Elizabeth said, giving her a warm, knowing smile. "I know that view from personal experience. Jacob and I love to take that same ride. In fact, it's the route he took me on when we were first falling in love. You might say it's the height of romance in Hart brothers' terms. If Isaac took you up there, he must've really wanted to impress you."

Tabitha nearly choked. "Oh, I don't think so. We're just friends. He's made that perfectly clear to me—on more than one occasion."

Elizabeth studied her for a moment before speaking.

"He's been... different since you and Caden arrived."

"Different, how?" Tabitha was almost afraid to ask.

"Less closed off, although I doubt anyone who doesn't live around him every day would think so, but it's true. You and Caden bring Isaac out of his shell the way no one else has been able to in a very long time."

Tabitha couldn't contain the small sound of disbelief that escaped her. "That's funny, because it seems like no matter what I say or do around him, it sends him running in the other direction."

Elizabeth smiled sympathetically. "He's not the most communicative man, I'll give you that. But give him time, Tabitha. Give him a little grace if you can. Things haven't been easy for Isaac, especially after what he's been through these past few years."

Tabitha frowned, her confusion deepening. "What do you mean?"

Elizabeth's eyes widened, as if she had realized too late

that she'd said too much. She hesitated, clearly weighing her next words with care. "I thought... I assumed Isaac would have told you."

"Told me what?" Tabitha's pulse quickened. Her heart dropped as she registered the look of deep sympathy in Elizabeth's expression. This was about whatever Isaac had been keeping from her all this time.

Elizabeth shifted in her chair, her mouth opening as if to speak, then closing as she reconsidered. "I don't want to overstep, especially if Isaac hasn't talked to you about this yet. It's not my place."

Tabitha's stomach twisted. Isaac hadn't opened up to her at all, not about his past, not about the things that weighed him down. She had sensed it, that dark cloud of grief hovering over him, but she didn't know the details, didn't understand why he kept retreating when they got close.

"It's fine," Tabitha murmured, her voice tight. "Isaac and I… well, maybe we aren't close enough for him to feel like he can share whatever this is."

Elizabeth's face softened with understanding. "It's not about you, Tabitha. Please don't think that."

Tabitha bit her lip, wanting to believe that, but the constant push and pull with Isaac made it hard. "It feels like it is. He lets me in just enough, and then it's like he shuts the door again. I don't know what I'm doing wrong."

Elizabeth reached out and gently touched Tabitha's hand. "You're not doing anything wrong. It's just that Isaac... he's been through a lot. More than most people know."

Tabitha stayed silent, waiting, her breath caught in her throat.

Elizabeth exhaled softly, her voice lowering as if what she

was about to say carried immense weight. "Isaac's wife, Anna, died three years ago in childbirth. The baby came early and there were complications. Isaac lost them both that day."

The terrible realization hit Tabitha like a physical blow. The air left her lungs on a jagged gasp as her hand flew to her mouth. Tears filled her vision then spilled down her cheeks. "Oh, no," she whispered. "I had no idea."

Elizabeth nodded, her own eyes glistening. "It broke him, Tabitha. Isaac was… shattered. He loved Anna deeply and losing her and their baby was like losing his whole world. He hasn't been the same since."

Tabitha blinked rapidly, trying to process what she was hearing. She could hardly breathe, her mind racing with the weight of it all. Isaac had been carrying this unimaginable grief, and she hadn't even known. He had never confided in her, never let her in far enough to understand.

"He must have been... devastated," Tabitha murmured, her voice shaking. "I can't even imagine."

Elizabeth's expression softened with empathy. "It's been hard for him to move on. He's still trying to figure out how to live with that pain, how to be... well, how to be whole again. But he's not very good at asking for help. I'm not sure he knows how to."

Tabitha wiped at a stray tear, feeling a pang of guilt. She had been so frustrated with Isaac for keeping his distance, for shutting her out—but now she understood why. He wasn't just running from her. He was running from his own heartache. And she couldn't blame him for that.

"He's never mentioned any of this to me," Tabitha whispered, the realization sinking deeper. "Not once."

Elizabeth squeezed her hand, her voice gentle but firm.

"That doesn't mean he doesn't care about you. He does, Tabitha. More than he lets on. I've seen the way he looks at you. I've seen the way he is around Caden. He's different when you're around."

Tabitha's heart ached. The puzzle pieces were beginning to fall into place, but that didn't make it easier to accept. Isaac's pain ran so deep, it had woven itself into the very fabric of who he was. How could she possibly compete with that kind of grief? How could she ask him to open up when it was clear he wasn't ready?

"I don't know what to do," Tabitha admitted, her voice barely above a whisper. "I care about him, but... he keeps pushing me away. I don't know if he'll ever be ready to let me in."

Elizabeth gave her a soft, reassuring smile. "It's not easy. Healing takes time, and Isaac... he's been through more than anyone should have to bear. But if you're patient, if you're willing to give him the space he needs, I believe he'll come around. He just needs to know that it's okay to let someone in again."

Tabitha exhaled, wiping at her eyes again. The idea of waiting, of giving Isaac the space to heal, both terrified her and gave her hope. She wanted to be there for him. But how long could she wait for him to open up, to let her in, to trust her with the pain of his past?

Elizabeth's gaze softened even more. "You should have all the information before you let yourself think that you're doing anything wrong where he's concerned." Elizabeth took a deep breath. "Although I never knew her, to hear Jacob describe it, Isaac's wife, Anna, wasn't just his love; she was his entire world. They were so excited to start a family, and when she died in childbirth... Isaac hasn't been the same since."

Tabitha felt a tear escape down her cheek. "I... I can't even imagine. Giving birth to Caden was one of the most incredible experiences of my life, but the joy..." She trailed off, the memory of holding her son for the first time filling her heart. She tried to picture the opposite—the loss, the despair—and it twisted her stomach into knots. "If I had lost him..."

"You'd never be the same, either" Elizabeth finished gently. "I don't think Isaac's incapable of moving forward. He just needs someone to remind him that there's still life, still happiness to be had, even after all the pain."

Tabitha wiped at her tears, shaking her head. "I just wish he'd tell me this himself. I wish he'd trust me enough to open up."

Elizabeth gave her hand a gentle squeeze. "Give him time. He's struggling with his own demons, but you've already gotten further with him than anyone else has in years. I know it's hard, but be patient with him, Tabitha. He's worth it."

A shout of glee from the pasture below brought Tabitha's attention back to the present. She dropped Elizabeth's hand and wiped a stray tear from her cheek.

"I better go down and meet Caden," Tabitha murmured. "They'll be done riding soon."

Elizabeth nodded, offering her a soft smile. "Take care, Tabitha. And don't give up on Isaac just yet."

Tabitha managed a faint smile and a nod, though her heart was heavy.

As she walked across the green pasture toward Caden and the other children, it all made a cold sort of sense. Isaac was grieving. He had lost his family all in one awful moment. No wonder he didn't want to move on or simply didn't know how. And Tabitha couldn't hold that against him.

But as much as she wanted to help him heal, she wasn't

sure if he'd ever be able—or willing—to let her be a part of that healing.

And that, more than anything, left her feeling utterly helpless.

CHAPTER 20

For three days in a row after his ride with Tabitha, Isaac made himself a promise every morning. He promised he would steer clear of her. He wouldn't be rude or purposely avoid her, but he also definitely wouldn't seek her out.

Each day, he broke that promise before noon.

The day after the ride, Tabitha had been sipping coffee in the ranch kitchen, chatting with a few others in the program, and Isaac couldn't help but join in. He had meant to grab coffee and leave, but he ended up sitting down, listening to them all discuss the pros and cons of other programs. He told himself it was to help the ranch improve its program for next time, but in truth, he was simply drawn to Tabitha, and her warm smile as she looked at him over the rim of her mug.

They had talked about the program's website, and Tabitha had offered to help redesign it, to make it more accessible and responsive. She even pulled her laptop from her bag to show Isaac examples of what she would do. He told himself he was listening to her ideas for the sake of the ranch, but he knew he leaned closer than necessary as she pointed at her screen and described all the ways they could improve the website.

That evening, they walked to the stables with Caden so he could meet Sunday. He was thrilled and impressed that his mother had ridden such a horse all by herself. So, Isaac insisted that Tabitha ride Sunday again the next day, with Caden sitting near Isaac by the paddock fence, clapping his hands as his mother and Sunday cantered in smooth circles.

Isaac knew his time with Tabitha and Caden wasn't going unnoticed, although no one made any comments. His mother was probably terrified that her remarks might draw him away from Tabitha, and Jacob was certainly unwilling to say anything after their first conversation on the subject. But they were all watching. They saw how he spent far more time outside his office. And while he had good intentions about keeping things cordial and friendly rather than romantic with Tabitha, somehow, he always ended up near her and Caden.

He was surprised to realize he no longer cared if anyone saw them together at the ranch. After all, they were friends. Hard as it was to remember that sometimes, especially when the memory of their kiss that night outside the guesthouse still lingered in his senses as if it had only been last night.

Tabitha certainly didn't seem inclined to bring anything up about it. She was being careful around him, too. She was her usual sunny self, but there was a slight reservation about her, as if she was holding herself at a distance as well.

He didn't know what he wanted when it came to Tabitha. He didn't know what he dared wish for where she was concerned. All he knew was, spending any bit of time with Tabitha was better than being without her.

That was why he had offered to take her and Caden to lunch in town. The kids had a free day to use however their parents wanted, and when Tabitha mentioned how much Caden liked eating at restaurants, Isaac told her he would drive them to the diner for lunch.

He waited in front of the ranch house for her, feeling awkward and nervous, as if he were taking Tabitha on a date. Even though it definitely wasn't that.

He was just enjoying the time he had with her. It was all temporary. In a matter of weeks, she would be gone, probably forever.

Then again, maybe she would return if they ever did the program again. The thought didn't fill Isaac with comfort, though. Instead, it was rather bleak to think about seeing her for a few weeks every year, and then saying goodbye. Each year, she would change, and Caden would grow taller, and Isaac would live off the brief glimpses of them. And someday Tabitha might show up with a new husband.

Isaac clenched his fists before quickly banishing that thought from his head. He had no right to think it. Never mind having any right to feel a surge of jealousy for an imaginary future man in her life. He would just enjoy the day he had ahead of him.

He heard Caden talking from around the corner before the boy and his mother came into sight. Caden ran ahead of Tabitha, his eyes bright with excitement as he shouted out Isaac's name.

Isaac tipped his hat at Caden, and Caden reached up to tip his own hat, just as he had been practicing since he first saw Isaac doing it.

Tabitha joined them, a soft smile on her face. She was wearing a loose short-sleeved white button-down over navy slacks. As always, she was dressed simply, yet she looked effortlessly elegant and sophisticated.

Isaac opened the door to his truck, helping Caden up into the cab while Tabitha installed the car seat. Tabitha had warned him quietly that Caden wouldn't like riding in the truck if it was messy. Isaac usually kept his vehicle neat, but he had gone over it this morning, clearing it of all the random pens and pieces of paper and ranch equipment, even vacuuming the seat.

Isaac held his breath as Caden sat in the middle seat, carefully surveying the new vehicle. When Caden seemed comfortable, Tabitha flashed Isaac a quick smile before climbing in and settling down next to Caden, helping him with his seat belt.

The drive to town was filled with Caden's happy chatter. He asked Isaac question after question about the truck and watched Isaac drive. The boy didn't miss a single detail.

Tabitha was quiet as she looked out the rolled-down window, the wind blowing her hair away from her face.

When they reached the diner, Isaac watched as a new sort of tension entered Tabitha's posture. He saw why she might be stressed. Caden could be a handful in a public space.

First, Caden wanted to carefully inspect every table before he chose one to sit at. Luckily, there were plenty of open tables, but even so, some of the customers cast them looks. Tabitha kept her head down as she focused on Caden, ignoring any stares. Isaac felt a burst of defensiveness that she was so used to being stared at in public.

He followed them as Caden counted the tables, then the stools, then sat at a booth before shaking his head due to the sun being in his eyes.

Finally, Caden opted for a booth and slid into the leather seat.

"Sorry." Tabitha grimaced as she looked at Isaac.

He reached out and touched her arm, guiding her into the seat across from Caden. "Don't apologize. We've got the best seat in the diner."

Tabitha's brows raised in surprise at the levity of Isaac's tone, and then she laughed. "I agree."

Caden insisted that Tabitha and Isaac read out every item on the menu two times as he deliberated.

Tabitha visibly relaxed as she realized Isaac wasn't growing impatient. As for Isaac, he was enjoying the whole thing. He hadn't been so happy to be eating at the diner in years, and he wanted the lunch to last as long as possible.

He was getting in too deep. He was getting too accustomed to being with both of them. They felt like their own unit.

And Isaac was remembering just how badly he had wanted this. Before he met Anna, even when he was young, he had known he wanted a family of his own. He had always pictured himself with children.

He was shocked to discover that he could still want that. That urge, buried deep inside him, had not vanished with his wife's death. It had simply been sleeping for a while.

After they finished their meal, they lingered at the table for way longer than necessary, Tabitha and Isaac chatting while Caden lined up the salt-and-pepper shakers and ketchup and mustard bottles in different patterns. He had an active mind, and he always needed something to focus on or else he got nervous.

The lunch lasted almost two hours, but Isaac was still sad when Tabitha announced they should probably head back.

Caden was fussy, too, wriggling between them in the truck.

"You need your nap, huh?" Tabitha asked.

Caden pouted. "No."

Tabitha cast Isaac a glance, as if she were nervous he would panic at the idea of Caden having a tantrum in his truck. Isaac gave her a calm smile, to reassure her it was all fine. He had known that Caden was different and might react to a sensory overload when he invited them to lunch. He didn't care about that.

"How many cows do you think we'll see on the way back to the ranch?" Isaac didn't know why he asked the question; he just thought it might be the type of thing Caden would think about.

Caden froze, his pout fading as he considered. "Maybe sixty?"

"I guess we better count to be sure," Isaac said.

Caden nodded, and for the rest of the ride, he was hyper-focused on counting the cows they saw along the highway.

He was still a bit grumpy when they arrived, but there was no meltdown, and Tabitha seemed relaxed and at ease.

Since she didn't make excuses to hurry away, Isaac walked them back to the guesthouse. And then, because Caden wanted to show him something in his room, Isaac ended up going inside with them, to the room where Caden slept. The bedroom Tabitha slept in was the next room over. Isaac tried not to picture her curled up on the big bed, her beautiful eyes closed in slumber, her soft curves warm and inviting beneath the quilt that covered the mattress.

Isaac was crossing a threshold, and he knew it. It was true, he had been in her room that first day, when he had carried her luggage in, but that was entirely different. Now he was where she and Caden were living. He was in their private space.

And he felt like somehow, he belonged.

He sat on Caden's bed as the boy showed him an array of

stuffed animals, all with names and precise places for them that Caden indicated.

He watched as Tabitha knelt down and helped Caden take off his boots, then his socks. Then Caden crawled under the blanket and curled up on his side.

"All right, I'll turn on your music."

Caden's eyes grew heavy as Tabitha put on quiet classical music on a speaker connected to her phone. Tabitha and Isaac headed for the door, and Isaac was pretty sure Caden was asleep as soon as they were in the hallway.

Tabitha moved down the hall, then she turned to Isaac and smiled. "He doesn't always go down that easily, but he was exhausted after the trip."

"Thank you for letting me take you." Isaac had sensed she was about to thank him, and he wanted to do it first. Because while she might think he was doing her favors, they were the ones doing so much more for him.

"We had a really good time." Tabitha leaned close to him.

Isaac couldn't stop himself. The house was quiet and empty, and he had wanted to kiss her for hours. When they were sitting side by side in the diner, he had felt the warmth of her body, and he had longed to stretch his arm around her shoulders and pull her tight against him.

He surrendered to that impulse now, moving before his brain told him all the reasons it was wrong to want her, wrong to crave her company and to wish they could have days like this one all the time. Brushing his lips over hers, he cupped her cheek in his hard palm and let his fingers delve into her silky dark hair.

Tabitha leaned into his kiss, her fingers resting against his chest. He placed his other hand at her hip to pull her against him.

Isaac's entire body was aflame. He wanted this. He wanted the cheerful lunches with Caden and Tabitha as a family. He wanted the quiet moments of listening to her and Caden discussing every random topic under the sun. He wanted to be the one to kiss Tabitha every evening and every morning.

He didn't know how he could have all that, not after everything he had been through, but he still wanted it.

Tabitha's hands turned firm against his torso, and she applied subtle but unmistakable pressure. She ducked her head as she gently pushed him away. Isaac pulled back instantly, appalled with himself.

"We shouldn't." Tabitha whispered her words to the wood planks at their feet. "I shouldn't be doing this, Isaac. I just..."

Her words broke off, and she slowly shook her head as she looked up at him. Isaac let his hands drop to his sides and took a step back. He didn't know what to do with his hands now that they were off Tabitha, so he crossed his arms. Tabitha copied his pose, a foot of space between them.

"I'm sorry." Guilt racked him. He knew he had been leading Tabitha on for days now. It hadn't been his intention. He wasn't leading her on now, with that kiss. He'd never wanted anything more than he wanted Tabitha back in his arms. "I'm sorry," he murmured. "I know I've been confusing."

She shook her head again. "I was confused, but now I'm not." Tabitha held his gaze, her eyes filled with sadness. Her jaw was set, though, as if she was determined to say something. "I'm going to be honest because I feel I have to. I know we agreed to be just friends, but I'm falling for you, Isaac. I have been for quite some time."

Isaac froze, his heart slamming against his ribcage as Tabitha's words hit him like a wave. She was falling for him.

He wanted to speak, to respond, but the truth was tangled up inside him, making it impossible to find the right words.

He had tried to deny how much he cared about her but hearing her confess her feelings stirred something deep inside him. He swallowed hard, his pulse racing. He wanted to reach for her again, to pull her back into his arms and tell her that he felt the same way.

"Tabitha, I—"

She held up a hand. "Please, let me say what I have to, Isaac. I care about you, but I have to protect myself because I don't want to get hurt." She wrapped her arms around her chest, as if she were trying to physically block him from reaching her heart. She glanced up at him, her eyes filled with fear. And pain. "I know about what happened to your family. To your wife and baby. Elizabeth told me by accident; she thought I already knew. Please, don't hold it against her."

Isaac's mind went blank. Tabitha knew. She knew about Anna and Alice and the hole deep inside him. That's why she knew she had to protect herself. She knew he could never give her what she deserved.

He didn't know what to feel, but he wasn't angry at Elizabeth. She had only said what he hadn't had the courage to do. She had only told Tabitha the truth, which was the least she deserved. He should have been the one to explain to Tabitha. Now, she was looking at him with a mixture of pity and tender caring that gutted him.

Isaac bowed his head and stared at the floorboards beneath his boots.

"I'm so sorry about everything." Tabitha's words were thick, as if she was holding back tears. "And I understand now. I really do. You don't owe me anything, I promise. We both have issues. We both have complications."

Isaac scoffed low under his breath. "You don't have issues. You're perfect, Tabitha. It's me who's messed up and broken."

"You're hurting," she corrected him softly. "That only means you're human, Isaac. The broken parts of you can heal... if you let them."

He knew she was right, despite how impossible it had been for him to accept that truth until now. Until he met her.

"I just wish—" Tabitha shook her head as if she didn't know how to finish the sentence. She cleared her throat. "I think you're a wonderful man, Isaac. And I'm so very sorry for what you've lost."

Her tender words slipped through Isaac's cracks and felt like a comforting blanket.

"I don't know how to be who I once was," he admitted, his voice low and rough. "I can't seem to live without a bone-jarring fear that nothing good lasts. Even if I could try to be with you, the whole time I would be scared of losing it all again."

Isaac had never been able to talk about his grief so openly, but it felt good to finally confess his feelings to Tabitha.

She reached out to him, placing her hand on his crossed arm. "I understand, and I can't imagine the pain you've been through. I don't know how I would cope if I suffered that kind of loss."

"Tabitha." Isaac took a deep breath and lifted his head. "I'm so sorry I can't be the person you want me to be."

She slowly shook her head. "I only ever wanted you to be yourself," Tabitha whispered. "But I understand that you're not ready."

"What if I was?" The question flew out of his mouth, only because he didn't want Tabitha to just walk away, to leave him forever. Somehow, he knew if she left him now, it was over.

Despite the feelings she had for him, she would be gone. She was right; she had to protect her heart too, and so far, all he'd been was a risk to her. "What if I am ready? Do you think maybe we could start over?"

Tabitha hesitated, her eyes searching his face. He could see the wariness in her gaze, the way she was trying to guard herself against the hope that was bubbling up between them. Slowly, she uncrossed her arms and let them fall to her sides.

"There's nothing I'd like more, but..." She trailed off, her voice soft. "Isaac, I can't be the one pulling you into something you're not sure about. I can't be the person waiting for you to figure out if you want this or not. I care about you, but I need to know that you're truly ready to let me in."

"I am," he said, his voice barely above a whisper. He stepped closer to her, unfolding his arms so he could touch Tabitha's face. "I know I've given you every reason to doubt me. I've never let anyone get close to me after Anna. I never thought I would. You've changed all that, Tabitha. You're changing me."

Tabitha's lips pressed together as she nodded. "You're changing me too. You've made me feel seen again, Isaac. You've made me long for things I thought I no longer wanted or needed. But I don't want to get hurt. I don't want Caden to get hurt if things don't work out for us."

"Of course," Isaac agreed, relief and guilt flooding him simultaneously. "Whatever you need. I just don't want to lose you."

Before either of them could say anything more, a voice called from down the hall. "Mom?"

Tabitha turned her head, her body tensing as Caden's voice floated down the hall from the bedroom.

"I should check on him," she murmured, her eyes flicking back to Isaac. "We'll talk more tomorrow?"

Isaac nodded, feeling an odd mixture of hope and uncertainty swirling inside him. "Yeah. Tomorrow."

Tabitha gave him a small, tentative smile before she headed toward Caden's room. Isaac watched her disappear into the bedroom, his heart feeling lighter than it had in a very long time.

The feeling was unfamiliar and strange, but he remembered it. Hope. That's what was pushing some of the shadows away from his heart. Hope, and love for the strong, patient woman who had blessed him with one more chance when he probably didn't deserve it.

Now that the air had been cleared between them, Isaac didn't want to leave. He wanted to stay and talk some more. Hold Tabitha in his arms for more than just a few scant moments.

But her son needed her more, so with the sounds of Tabitha's soothing voice murmuring in the bedroom down the hall, Isaac turned around and left her to look after her child.

CHAPTER 21

The next morning, Tabitha stood at the fence and watched Caden trot in a full circle around the paddock. His posture was straight, and his smile stretched wide as he followed the instructor's guidance. Every time Caden looked over at her, she gave him a reassuring wave, her heart swelling with pride. He was coming so far, gaining confidence with every passing day, and that alone made her time at the ranch worth it.

But even as she focused on Caden, her thoughts kept drifting back to the conversation she'd had with Isaac the night before. His kiss, his apology, the way he'd confessed to feeling afraid of losing everything again—all of it had left her reeling. She had sensed for weeks that Isaac was holding something back but hearing him speak so openly about his fear of getting hurt, about his grief and loss, made everything feel more real.

She had admitted her own feelings to him, but she was still guarded. The man she was falling for was still haunted by his past. They had agreed to start over, to try—but what did that mean? Was she setting herself up for heartbreak? Could she really trust him to open up fully and let her in?

As much as she wanted to believe in the possibility of a future with Isaac, doubts lingered. What would happen when the program ended? She couldn't ask him to leave the ranch. It was his home, his family's legacy. And could she really uproot her and Caden's life to move closer to a man who wasn't yet sure if he could truly commit?

She shook her head, trying to clear her mind as footsteps approached from behind. Turning, she saw Vera walking toward her, the older woman waving a hand in greeting before stopping beside her.

"Beautiful day, isn't it?" Vera smiled up at the sky, blue and clear.

Tabitha returned her smile, though her thoughts were still elsewhere. "It is."

"I saw your email this morning with your ideas for the website redesign. I'm impressed." Vera's tone was genuine, and Tabitha felt a small flicker of pride.

"Thanks," Tabitha replied, shifting her weight. She hadn't been able to sleep after her conversation with Isaac. After reading a story to Caden to help him fall asleep, she'd stayed up late working on the new website mockup for the horsemanship program. It had been a welcome mental distraction, and she had wanted to do it. It felt like the best way she could show her gratitude for everything the program had done for Caden.

"You have to charge us for it." Vera's tone was blunt and firm. "It's too good, far better than we might have found on our own."

Tabitha shook her head, even as she noticed the determined set to Vera's jaw. "No, truly, it's a gift. I'm happy to do it."

Vera pursed her lips, her expression softening slightly, though her resolve was clear. "Well, you're good at what you do, that's for sure. I'm tempted to offer you a job handling all our online presence."

Tabitha blinked, caught off guard by the offer. There was a warmth in Vera's voice, but there was something else, too—an underlying sincerity that made Tabitha realize the woman wasn't joking. For a moment, the thought of staying in Wyoming, working at the ranch, even being closer to Isaac, flickered through her mind. But she quickly pushed it aside. "I'm sure there's someone local who could help you out."

"Maybe," Vera said with a small shrug, though the look in her eyes said otherwise. "But I doubt anyone local has your skill set. And this place—it's not just the horsemanship program that needs a boost. We've been talking for a while about expanding our online presence for the ranch. Rentals, lessons, maybe even a small online store for local goods. We're falling behind, and it's the way the world works now. We need to catch up."

Tabitha crossed her arms and nodded. "It is. I can't complain, though. It's what keeps me with plenty of work."

"I imagine so." Vera studied her for a long moment, her gaze thoughtful. "You know, this place could use someone like you. Someone with vision, who understands both the business side and the personal connections that matter in a place like this."

Tabitha looked away, feeling a slight pang in her chest. Vera was being kind, but the idea of staying here, of making Wyoming her home, felt overwhelming. It wasn't just about the work. It was about Isaac, about Caden. Could she really ask her son to uproot his life, move away from California and the support system they had there, for a man who wasn't sure if he could let go of his past?

"I appreciate the offer, Vera. Really, I do." Tabitha's voice was soft. "But my life, my work—it's all back in California."

Vera tilted her head, her gaze warm but probing. "Is it? I mean, don't get me wrong, I know you've built a life there. But you've also found something here. Something that feels... good, doesn't it?"

Tabitha swallowed, her throat suddenly tight. Vera was right. There was something about this place—about the ranch, about Isaac—that felt right. But the uncertainty gnawed at her. Could she really take that leap? Could she trust Isaac enough to start over with him, knowing he still hadn't fully let go of his grief?

"I don't know," Tabitha admitted, her voice barely above a whisper. "It does feel good here. But... it's complicated."

Vera nodded, her expression understanding. "Of course, it is. But sometimes the best things in life are the ones that scare us a little, the ones that make us question everything."

Tabitha exhaled slowly, her gaze drifting back to Caden, who was now laughing as his horse trotted across the paddock. She wanted to be hopeful. She wanted to believe that she and Isaac could make things work, that they could build something together. But the doubts wouldn't leave her alone.

She could never ask Isaac to leave Hart's Ridge Ranch. This was his home, his family's legacy. And what about her and Caden? Uprooting their life to move here felt... risky. It wasn't just her decision—Caden's well-being came first, and she couldn't make a choice that would throw his world into chaos, not for a relationship that wasn't guaranteed.

Vera reached out and touched her arm gently, breaking through her thoughts. "You don't have to decide today. Just take it one step at a time. You'll figure out what's best for you and Caden. And if that means staying here, well... this ranch has a way of working its way into people's hearts."

After a moment, Vera gave Tabitha's arm a reassuring squeeze before stepping back. "I'll let you get back to your morning. But just know, if you ever need anything—or someone to talk to—I'm here."

"Thank you, Vera." Tabitha smiled softly, feeling a warmth from the older woman's offer.

Vera nodded and then turned to walk away, her boots kicking up soft puffs of dust as she headed toward the main house. Tabitha remained at the fence, her fingers lightly gripping the weathered wood as she watched Caden trot in a circle around the paddock, his laughter brightening the morning air as Ben led Caden's horse at an easy gait.

The peaceful scene should have calmed her, but her thoughts kept drifting back to Isaac. She wasn't sure what the day ahead would bring, or how they would move forward, but the pull between them was undeniable. She could feel it in the way he looked at her—like he wanted to be closer, but was still figuring out how to let himself take that step.

Movement from the stables caught her eye, and she turned to see Isaac standing with Mateo. Their conversation seemed easy, casual, but the moment Isaac saw her, his expression softened. Their gazes locked, and the connection was instant —an unspoken understanding passing between them. It was as if they were the only two people in the world for a moment, the ranch fading into the background.

Her heart fluttered, and she couldn't help but wonder what today might bring. There was so much left to be said, but the way he looked at her now made her hopeful. The tenderness in his eyes told her he hadn't changed his mind about trying. They both wanted this. They just had to figure out how to make it work.

She smiled softly in return, feeling that familiar warmth spread through her chest. But just as quickly, her attention shifted when she noticed something was off in the paddock.

Most of the counselors were gathered around another boy, Luke, who seemed to have had an issue dismounting. Donna was in one corner, Molly a few feet away, both of them mounted on horses. Ben stood nearby the women, gripping the halter of the horse he had been leading, his attention focused on whatever was happening with Luke.

But Ben's horse had no rider.

Caden wasn't there now.

Tabitha's heart skipped a beat, her body jolting with sudden alarm. She shot to her feet, her eyes scanning the paddock frantically. Where was Caden?

Her gaze darted from one end of the ring to the other, but there was no sign of him. She whirled around, searching the area beyond the paddock, looking toward the lawn and the path that led toward the main house. Had he wandered off while she was busy mooning over Isaac? How had she let herself lose sight of her child so easily?

"Caden?" she called, her voice rising with urgency as she tried to keep the panic from flooding her system.

That feeling of dread worsened in the next breath.

Because she realized then that Caden had somehow gotten off his horse unnoticed and walked out of the training paddock. He had ambled across the green pasture.

And he had ducked under the fence to a nearby holding pen.

Inside the pen was a mare that Tabitha only wished she didn't recognize.

Maeve. The newly purchased mare. She was one of the horses everyone had been warned to stay away from. She was the mare with the black coat that Tabitha had admired in the stables before Isaac took her on their ride. He had said that Maeve was basically untrained. And skittish.

In desperation, Tabitha looked around for Diane or Beau or any other employee at the ranch who might be able to get Caden away from that horse's hooves. There was no one. Caden was looking up at an easily spooked horse, and no one was even close to him.

He was only a few feet away from the animal, and Maeve had stiffened, her black coat gleaming in the sun over her tensed muscles.

"Caden." Tabitha kept her voice low. Tabitha started to speed walk toward her son, but even as she moved, she knew she was too far to stop the inevitable. She wanted to shriek his name, but she knew that would be bad. Maeve might jolt at the sound, and Caden was just as likely to lurch closer to the horse as he was to get out of the pen. Even if he moved fast, he couldn't outrun a horse. Not if Maeve moved in fear.

She would trample him. Tabitha felt her hands shake as she watched her son, who looked so very small, take another step toward the horse.

He didn't know. The entire program, he had been around gentle and docile animals. He had no idea that Maeve was any different.

Tabitha only had eyes for Caden, but she felt the wave of tension in the air as everyone else noticed what had happened.

She was almost past the paddock, still half a soccer field

from Caden, but she heard a muffled curse from one of the counselors before a silence descended over the others.

It was her fault. Tabitha knew that as her entire world slowed down.

She should have been watching Caden. Yes, he had been with the counselors, but she was his mother. She should have had her eyes on him every second.

Instead, she had been distracted by Isaac and wrapped up in her own feelings. Tabitha had ignored her son because her foolish heart was tangled up in a man. And now her son was about to be hurt. Or far worse.

Tabitha's mind went blank. She couldn't even think. She couldn't even imagine an existence without Caden.

Even from so far away, Tabitha saw Maeve's eye roll back so that the whites showed.

It was a sign ingrained in Tabitha when she was a little girl. Her father had taught her how to read the language of horses. When they showed the whites of their eyes, they were startled or unsure. Maeve clearly wasn't used to people, and she definitely was unused to small boys approaching her in her holding pen.

Her front knees bent, and her lethal hooves scuffed against the ground.

Somehow, Caden seemed to sense that something was wrong, even though he hadn't learned as Tabitha had. He went still and backed up a step.

But it was too late. Tabitha knew it was too late.

Maeve was about to rear up on her hind legs, and when she came down, she would come down hard. Anything nearby would be trampled.

Tabitha could no longer remain calm. She felt a scream rising in her throat. Behind her, she sensed movement, as if the others were moving with her toward the pen, but no one could run that fast.

Just as Tabitha was about to go into hysterics, movement from the side of Maeve's pen caught her eye.

Tabitha froze. It was Isaac. Somehow, some way, he had reached the pen from where he had been standing by the stables. He must have seen Caden before anyone else. While Tabitha was frantically scanning the area for her little boy, Isaac must have been watching Caden and leaped into action. He had seen her son when she had been unable to.

The world seemed to go perfectly still. All thought left Tabitha's head, and all she could do was watch.

Caden was stumbling away, and Maeve was scuffing her hooves into the dirt, but Isaac alone was calm. A pillar of composure.

He was standing by the fence, reaching out his arm.

"Caden." Isaac's voice was so low, it barely reached Tabitha's ears, but she could hear him. She was stunned at how steady his words were. "Caden, take my hand."

And Caden, who never trusted people he didn't know well, who only let Tabitha or therapists he had worked with for years touch him, and only under specific circumstances, instantly threw himself at Isaac's strong and capable hands.

In one smooth movement, Isaac had pulled Caden toward the fence, gripped him under his arms, and hoisted him up and over to safety.

A millisecond later, Maeve let out a loud neigh as she reared up on her hind legs and then brought her front hooves pounding back to earth. Right where Caden had been moments before.

Tabitha clapped her hand over her mouth. She almost fell to her knees as relief coursed through her.

Isaac didn't even flinch as Maeve continued to rear; he simply turned and carried Caden away.

Tabitha saw Mateo step toward the fence, his arms spread wide as he murmured to the horse. Then Beau came sprinting from the direction of the stables, his eyes wide with panic.

"What on earth, Beau?" Mateo snapped at his brother. "Why was Maeve unsupervised?"

"I thought Leroy was out here." Beau was gasping for breath, and he clearly felt terrible about the entire situation.

Tabitha didn't care about that drama, though. She only had eyes for her son.

She ran toward Isaac, and time seemed to unfreeze and speed up.

Tabitha crashed into the both of them, and then Caden had his arms around her, his face pressed into her neck. She held him tight, and her chest heaved with dry sobs as she sucked in air.

Her eyes found Isaac, but she couldn't seem to speak.

He didn't step away, though. He stayed standing close, his hands on her shoulders. "It's okay, Tabitha, he's safe. Just breathe."

With Caden held tightly against her chest, Tabitha kept her eyes locked on Isaac, and slowly, bit by bit, the raw panic seeped out of her.

"It's okay, it's okay. I promise." Isaac's hands moved over her shoulders, his murmured words wrapping around her as warm and strong as his arms.

And then they were surrounded by everyone else.

"Tabitha, I'm sorry. I don't know what happened." Donna's face was etched with fear, and all the counselors wore similar expressions.

Ben looked like he was about to hurl himself under

Maeve's hooves out of guilt. "It was my fault. I got distracted. I'm so sorry."

Vera arrived too, stomping past the knot of people surrounding Tabitha, her eyes fixed on her youngest son. Once she reached Beau, she started talking to him in an undertone, and Tabitha knew she was not mincing her words by the way Beau hung his head in shame.

"It's okay." Tabitha looked at Donna and Ben first, since they seemed the most upset. "Everyone makes mistakes, and I'm the one who should have been paying closer attention."

Caden began to squirm and let out a huff, and Tabitha realized it was getting too crowded. He was going to be over-stimulated and overwhelmed.

As if he could read her thoughts, Isaac placed one hand on Tabitha's back and held up the other to keep people away as he guided Tabitha out of the crowd and back toward the paddock.

Tabitha set Caden down and knelt beside him. "Are you okay, honey?"

Caden nodded, but Tabitha could tell he was close to tears.

"Let's go to the house where it's quiet, okay?" Tabitha stood and smiled with relief as Caden gripped her hand. "We'll have some water."

"Will Isaac come?"

Tabitha was speechless. She shouldn't have been surprised, though. Caden had demonstrated a remarkable sense of trust when he had reached for Isaac. And Isaac had shown he could be calm and levelheaded in the direst of situations.

Tabitha didn't know how she could ever thank him enough. She looked up at him, prepared to ask if he minded, but Isaac spoke before she could.

"Of course, I'm right behind you two." Isaac acted as if it

were just another day. His veneer of composure put both Tabitha and Caden at ease.

She guided Caden toward the main house, and her attention was on her son, but she felt Isaac's presence behind her the entire walk.

Once they reached the house, Tabitha's heart finally returned to its normal rhythm. She let Caden choose where he wanted to sit down. He opted for the wide leather couch in the living room, and Tabitha helped Caden climb onto the middle cushion, his favorite spot on any couch.

Before she could even ask, Isaac was handing water, in a plastic bottle, as Caden preferred, to her son as well as her.

Caden clutched his water, but he didn't drink. He stared straight ahead as Tabitha crouched beside him. Her heart ached. Her son was clearly in shock.

"Mommy, I was really scared." His boyish voice was so small that Tabitha almost started crying right then and there.

"So was I, Caden," Tabitha said. "You should never go up to a horse you don't know, all alone, okay?"

Caden's face crumbled, and Tabitha knew he was upset. She didn't want to chastise him after such a frightening moment, but she also knew she had to make him understand what he'd done was risky. She had to teach him not to do such a thing again.

Only she had no idea how to impart that lesson without making Caden feel ashamed or punished.

"You were scared, and so was the horse." Isaac sat in the armchair across from Caden. His tone was firm but far from cruel. In fact, he was smiling at Caden in a reassuring way. "When you get scared, you sometimes scream or throw things, right? Horses are the same. They can get nervous, just like we do, only instead of screaming, horses kick. So that's why you always have to be careful."

Caden stared at Isaac and nodded as the man's words sank in.

Tabitha's heart squeezed hard in her breast as she watched the man she loved comfort her child as if Caden were his own.

Isaac didn't know how much Caden already looked up to him. If he did know the extent of Caden's adoration and love, Isaac could have doubts about his ability to be a father again.

After the most terrifying moment of her life, her son was safe. As long as Caden was alive and well, Tabitha could consider herself the luckiest woman in the world.

And then there was Isaac.

She lifted her eyes to him, and she almost couldn't breathe at the sight of him. She had loved him before, but after what he had just done, her love had multiplied tenfold.

"Thank you," she said, moving onto the couch next to her son. "Thank you so much."

He smiled and gave her a warm nod. "I'm glad I was there. For you, and for Caden."

"Me too," she admitted softly.

A deeply sober look seeped into Isaac's tender gaze. "Can we talk, Tabitha? We haven't had a chance to finish our conversation from last night, and I've been doing a lot of thinking in the time since. I have something I need to say to you."

The utter seriousness in his voice put a different kind of worry in her heart. Was Isaac having second thoughts about her? Had she read him all wrong again? Heaven help her, she didn't know if she could bear another bump in their relationship—especially not now.

"Um," Tabitha hedged, looking at Caden, who had climbed off the couch and was now happily gulping down his water where he sat on the rug-covered floor.

"When you're ready," Isaac clarified. "I just—I need to ask you something."

Tabitha furrowed her brow in confusion, but before she could answer, her friend Cindy entered the room with a few of the counselors, flanked by Vera.

Isaac's mother headed straight to Tabitha, her face fraught with regret. "Tabitha, I am so sorry. That should never have happened."

"Please, don't blame yourself." Tabitha had been scared, but she knew it was an honest mistake. Things like this happened. She wasn't going to act like she had been watching Caden every second. "And truly, Isaac was so levelheaded and quick on his feet. He knew exactly what to do. I owe him everything."

Isaac seemed suddenly uncomfortable with both Tabitha's praise and the extra people in the room. He nodded once before getting to his feet and quietly leaving the room.

Vera continued to apologize profusely, and Cindy took a seat by Tabitha's side. Tabitha took her friend's hand. Cindy had obviously been just as shaken by the entire event.

An hour later, Caden had rejoined the other kids for a tutoring session. Tabitha had asked if he wanted to go back to the guesthouse or stay by her side, but he had insisted on continuing with his day. Tabitha sensed nothing would make him feel better after being so badly rattled than returning to the routine, so she let him go with the counselors. Fortunately, they were scheduled for indoor activities for the rest of the day. Tabitha's heart couldn't have withstood letting Caden back outside or near the horses so quickly.

Vera had assured Tabitha that she would be taking steps to heighten the caution and horse-handling practices, and that she now knew for sure she should hire even more counselors for the next program. She had also offered Tabitha a full refund half a dozen times, which Tabitha kept rejecting. She would take a discount if it would make Vera feel better, but Tabitha didn't want to act as if the program was completely worthless because of an isolated incident.

"We got complacent," Vera said, with a shake of her head. "Because nothing like that happened in the first few weeks, people let down their guard. It won't happen again. I promise you that."

Tabitha believed her, and she told her as much. At last, Vera headed out to the stables, probably to scold Beau and the other trainers some more. That, Tabitha couldn't complain about.

She was glad to be alone at last in the quiet ranch house. She leaned back on the couch, her body suddenly exhausted after the whirlwind of emotions.

A footstep in the doorway startled her from her daze.

It was Isaac, holding a mug. He hadn't left. Apparently, he had just been waiting for the bustle to die down.

He walked over to Tabitha and handed her the mug. She took it wordlessly. It was tea with milk, just the way she preferred it.

She should have been on edge at his presence. She had been nervous and jumpy for days, even when he was at a distance.

Instead, Tabitha only felt calm. This man, she would trust with everything. Even her heart, which was his completely, whether he wanted it or not.

Right now, given his solemn demeanor as he looked at her,

she was afraid to guess what was weighing so heavily on his mind.

Isaac sat down on the couch next to her, his expression steady but intense, his eyes searching hers.

He leaned forward, resting his elbows on his knees, and drew a deep breath. "Tabitha, I've been struggling," he began quietly, his voice rough with emotion. "Not because I don't care about you. I do. More than I know how to explain. But I've been confused—about everything. About what I'm feeling for you and for Caden. And I've been afraid. Afraid of letting myself believe I could have this again. A life with someone. A family."

Her heart ached at the vulnerability in his words. Isaac wasn't the kind of man to bare his soul easily, but here he was, laying it all out in front of her.

"I've been trying to keep my distance, convincing myself it's for the best." He paused, his jaw tightening briefly before he continued. "But after today... after last night... After spending these past few weeks around you and trying to keep myself from admitting everything I'm feeling for you, I realized I don't want to keep pretending. I can't go on lying to myself, or, more importantly, to you. I can't keep denying what I feel for you."

Emotion filled her chest, making it hard to breathe and impossible to form words. His confession stirred a flood of feelings within her—hope, love, and the same fear that mirrored his. Her mind raced, processing everything he was saying, while a storm of tangled emotions swirled inside her.

Isaac's gaze was unwavering, his hands clasped together as if he was bracing himself for whatever response she might give. "I know I haven't made things easy," he admitted, his voice growing softer. "But I don't want to run from this anymore. From us. Because I love you, Tabitha."

CHAPTER 22

She didn't say anything.

Isaac thought it would be difficult to say the words he'd needed to say to Tabitha, but to his astonishment, telling her that he loved her was the easiest thing in the world for him to do.

The moment those words left his mouth, it was as if a weight had been lifted from his chest. For the first time in what felt like forever, he wasn't hiding behind the walls he'd built around himself. He wasn't running from his emotions.

But now, as the silence stretched between them, a different kind of tension gripped him.

Her eyes, wide and filled with emotions he couldn't quite decipher, stayed locked on his. She hadn't moved, hadn't blinked, and he suddenly wondered if he'd misread everything. Was she in shock? Was she… afraid?

"Tabitha," he began, his voice softer now, almost pleading. "I know I've kept you at arm's length. I've been afraid of everything these feelings stirred up, afraid of dragging you into the mess my life had become. But that doesn't mean I don't want this. I do. More than I can explain."

She still didn't speak, her gaze flickering away from his face to somewhere in the room, her lips parted slightly as if searching for words. The silence gnawed at him. What was she thinking? Did she feel the same? Or had his confession thrown her off balance?

Isaac shifted in his seat, the raw vulnerability coursing through him making him feel exposed. "I don't expect you to say anything back," he added hastily, as if trying to offer her a way out. "I just needed you to know how I feel—about you and Caden."

Tabitha's gaze shot back to his, the mention of her son striking a chord. Isaac felt the need to explain further, needing her to understand just how deep his feelings ran.

"I care about him too," Isaac said quietly. "Caden's special. I know I don't need to tell you that. But being around him has shown me things I thought I'd never feel again. He's helped me realize that I still want a family. That I still have room in my heart for that kind of love."

His throat tightened as he continued, "I know this hasn't been easy for you, and I've made it harder by holding back. But I'm here now. I'm ready, Tabitha, if you'll have me."

For a long, excruciating moment, Isaac waited. Watched her, studied her every little movement, every flicker of emotion that crossed her face. He couldn't read her, and it was killing him.

Finally, Tabitha let out a breath and turned to him, her eyes shining with unshed tears. But still, she didn't speak.

"Please, just say something," Isaac whispered, his voice rough, his heart pounding against his ribs. He wasn't sure how long he could handle the silence between them.

Tabitha's lips parted as she inhaled a shaky breath. She finally found her voice, though it came out small and trembling. "Isaac... I'm in love with you too." She paused, as if the admission itself cost her something. "But I'm afraid. I'm afraid of how deeply I've fallen in love with you in such a short time."

Isaac's breath caught. He hadn't known what to expect, but hearing her echo his feelings sent a wave of warmth—and relief—through him.

Yet her next words stopped his heart cold.

"I worry, Isaac, because what if you wake up one day and realize that Caden and I are too much? That we're not what you want. We're not easy, either one of us. We aren't perfect."

He frowned. "I've never wanted or needed perfect. Lord knows, I'm far from it myself."

She smiled tenderly. "But you've been through so much. You deserve—" Her voice broke. "After everything you've lost, Isaac, you deserve an easy life with a perfect family."

Isaac shook his head, his chest tight with a mix of frustration and tenderness. "Tabitha, listen to me. The one thing I've never been afraid of is hard work. That's not what scares me. I've spent my whole life working the land, doing things that are tough. But nothing about loving you... nothing about loving Caden is hard for me. It never will be. Loving both of you is the easiest thing I've ever done."

Tabitha's eyes slowly met his, filled with uncertainty.

He edged closer to her, gently taking her hands in his. "That moment in the paddock... seeing Caden so close to danger, I thought my heart was going to stop. I've never felt fear like that before." He paused, his thumb tracing soothing circles on her skin. "But it made me realize something. You and Caden—you're already my family. I'd do anything to protect you, to keep you safe."

Tabitha swallowed hard, tears shimmering in her eyes as she listened, her expression softening.

"I know I've been guarded, and I haven't made this easy for you," Isaac continued, his voice rough with emotion. "But my feelings for you and Caden? That's never going to change. You and Caden will be my family even if you go home to California after the program is over."

He squeezed her hand, his heart pounding in his chest. "I love you both, and I'll love you whether you're a thousand miles away or right here on this ranch. What I'm trying to say is, I don't want you to leave. Not after the program ends. Not ever. I want you and Caden to stay. I want us to build a life together… if you'll have me."

Before she could respond, Isaac took a deep breath and moved off the couch. He knelt down in front of her, his eyes never leaving hers. "In case there's any doubt in your mind, Tabitha Young, you are the only woman I want. I know I don't have a ring right now," he said, his voice soft, "but I promise I'll make good on that. I'll make good on all the things you deserve."

"Isaac," she whispered, tears spilling over the rims of her beautiful eyes. He held her glistening gaze. "Tabitha, I love you. I love Caden too. The only future I want is one that includes both of you. Will you marry me?"

CHAPTER 23

Tabitha's heart raced, and her breath caught as she listened to Isaac's words. He loved her. He loved Caden, too. And wanted them to stay at Hart's Ridge Ranch with him—forever,

It wasn't until that moment that she'd actually allowed herself to imagine her life as a part of the Hart family. She and Caden making their home with Isaac at his family's ranch. The place already felt like home to them both. Caden had never been happier anywhere, and as for her, Tabitha couldn't think of anywhere she'd rather be than right there with Isaac.

As his wife.

This man, this kind, honorable man, who had captured her heart from the beginning and had shown nothing but kindness to Caden—this wounded man, who had held himself back for so long to protect his own heart—was now baring it to her, promising her everything she'd dreamed of but feared she'd never find.

In her lengthening silence, Isaac's tender gaze grew hesitant. He glanced down at their loosely clasped hands. "You don't have to answer right now, Tabitha. I know this is a lot. If you need some time to think about it—"

"I don't need more time, Isaac."

His eyes lifted once more, locking on hers. He swallowed. "You don't?"

A tear slipped down her cheek as she shook her head, barely able to speak through the rush of her emotions. "My answer is yes," she whispered, her voice breaking with joy. "Yes, Isaac. I will marry you."

Isaac's face broke into a warm, relieved smile, his eyes bright with devotion as he pulled her into his arms.

Their kiss was soft, lingering, a quiet seal to everything they had shared and everything that lay ahead. She felt the warmth of his hand on her back, grounding her, as if he could hold her forever and still not be close enough.

Just then, the sound of footsteps and voices carried from the hallway, and they turned to see Caden, chattering animatedly as he walked in with Vera. Caden's eyes lit up as he spotted them, and he bounded into the room. Vera paused, taking in the scene with a warm but questioning smile, clearly sensing that something had happened.

"Oh, I'm sorry to interrupt," she said, her voice gentle, though her eyes sparkled with curiosity. "We just came in for a little snack."

Before Tabitha could respond, Caden tilted his head, noticing her tear-streaked cheeks. His brows knit together in concern. "Mom? Why are you crying?" He looked quickly between her and Isaac, his small face a mixture of confusion and worry.

Tabitha let out a soft laugh and knelt beside him, brushing her hands through his hair. "Oh, sweetheart, these are happy tears." She glanced at Isaac, her eyes warm. "We have some special news to tell you."

Caden's brow furrowed as he tried to understand, glancing up at Isaac and then back to his mom. Isaac crouched beside them, meeting Caden at eye level. His face softened as he reached for the boy's shoulder. "Caden, I asked your mom to marry me," he said gently, watching as the words sank in.

Vera's hands flew to her mouth, a delighted gasp escaping her lips. "Oh, Isaac!"

Caden's eyes went wide as he processed Isaac's words, his gaze darting from his mom to Isaac and back again. He looked up at Isaac, a glimmer of understanding and wonder shining in his eyes. "Does that mean… you're gonna be my dad?" he asked, his voice tentative but filled with hope.

Isaac's smile was full of warmth as he nodded. "Only if that's all right with you, buddy." Caden's face broke into a wide grin, and before either Isaac or Tabitha could react, he threw his arms around Isaac's neck, holding on tight. "Yes!" he said, his voice muffled as he buried his face against Isaac's shoulder.

Tabitha's heart swelled, overcome by her son's unabashed joy and the certainty in his embrace. It was as though every doubt she'd had about bringing Caden into this new life, every fear she'd harbored about whether they truly belonged here, vanished in that single moment. Here, surrounded by Isaac's strength and Caden's innocence, she felt the peace she had been searching for.

Isaac tightened his hold on Caden, then pulled Tabitha close, wrapping an arm around her as well. She felt herself smile through more tears as she leaned into their embrace, the three of them together, finally.

Vera beamed as she looked on, her eyes bright with tears

of her own. "Well, this will be an extra special supper tonight," she announced, clapping her hands. "I can't wait to celebrate this news with everyone!"

Caden wiggled out of their embrace and tugged on Vera's hand. "Now, you're crying. Are those happy tears too?"

Vera glanced briefly at Tabitha and her son before turning her gentle gaze on Caden. "Yes, they sure are, sweetheart. You know why?"

He shook his head.

"Because this exciting news also means I'm going to be your grandmother." Vera winked at Tabitha and Isaac. "Hopefully sooner than later."

Tabitha laughed as Isaac pulled her close, wrapping her under the sheltering strength of his arm. "Didn't I hear something about a snack?"

"Yes!" Instantly distracted by the idea of a treat, Caden hopped up and down and took hold of Vera's hand. "Let's go now!"

Isaac's mom smiled indulgently as she allowed Caden to pull her into the kitchen.

Her laughter echoed down the hallway as they left, and Isaac and Tabitha shared a warm, quiet smile, grateful for the peace that settled around them in the now-empty room.

Once they were alone, Isaac drew her back to him for another kiss.

"I see what you did there," she joked, looking up at him as their lips parted. "Evidently, your expert wrangling skills extend beyond the horse paddock."

"Yes, ma'am." He chuckled, and the sound rumbled against her. It was good to hear him laugh. It was good to see him smile at her son and care for him with the kind of gentle, fatherly affection Caden had never known.

Until now.

Until Isaac Hart stepped into their lives... and into their hearts.

With a soft sigh, Tabitha leaned into him, resting her cheek against his chest, savoring the feel of his heartbeat beneath her. He tilted her face toward his, his thumb brushing lightly over her cheek as he met her gaze, and in that moment, nothing else mattered.

"Thank you," he whispered into her hair, his voice rough with emotion. "Thank you for trusting me, Tabitha. For giving me another chance at love. At a family."

Tabitha reached up, gently touching his face. "Thank you for being everything I didn't even know I was waiting for. I love you so much, Isaac."

He caressed her cheek. "I love you too."

They kissed again, and in that quiet moment, their future felt as sure and as endless as the warmth they held between them. Here, in each other's arms, they had everything they needed—and a lifetime to share it.

A NOTE FROM THE AUTHOR

I hope you enjoyed Isaac and Tabitha's story! If you did, please consider writing a brief review where you purchased the book to share your thoughts with other readers. I would also be very grateful if you left a review for the book at BookBub or Goodreads. Thank you for all your support!

Now that you've read the fifth book in the Cowboy Brothers of Hart's Ridge Ranch series, I hope you'll watch for the next novel in the series.

Be sure to sign up for my website newsletter to stay updated on my new releases!

Join My Reader List

Get the prequel to the **Cowboy Brothers of Hart's Ridge Ranch** series for FREE when you sign up for my reader email list! You'll also be the first to learn about my books, special content, promotions, and more.

FaithLandon.com

BOOKS BY FAITH LANDON

Her Cowboy's Hopeful Heart (series prequel)

Her Cowboy's Reluctant Heart

Her Cowboy's Irresistible Heart

Her Cowboy's Untamed Heart

Her Cowboy's Faithful Heart

Her Cowboy's Wounded Heart

MORE TO COME!

ABOUT THE AUTHOR

Hi! I'm Faith Landon, and I love writing sweet, contemporary cowboy romances. I adore anything set in the American West, and when I'm not writing, you can usually find me watching Hallmark Christmas movies or reading a good romance novel.

My favorite reads are clean and wholesome romances that feature lots of family, heartwarming romance, and happy endings that leave me with a smile on my face for days after turning the last page. That's also what I strive to write in my own novels.

Please visit my website to learn more about me and my books. **Be sure to sign up** for my reader email list while you're there! I'll send you the prequel story to the Cowboy Brothers of Hart's Ridge Ranch series, **Her Cowboy's Hopeful Heart**, as a gift for subscribing.

Visit me at
FaithLandon.com

facebook.com/FaithLandonAuthor
bookbub.com/authors/faith-landon
goodreads.com/FaithLandon
pinterest.com/FaithLandonAuthor

Made in the USA
Las Vegas, NV
21 November 2024